MR TIGER,
BETSY
and the
SEA DRAGON

MR TIGER,
BETSY
and the
SEA DRAGON

Sally Gardner

illustrated by
Nick Maland

ZEPHYR

An imprint of Head of Zeus

To Amelia Barratt, with all my love
— SG

For Susie and David, with love
— NM

There is an island that has been left off the map of the world. It is here that the letters of the alphabet come from. As every story starts with words and as every word is made up of letters, it is only fair and two corners square that the letters of the alphabet tell this one in their own words.

It started on a stormy day when the rain danced shiny over the decks of

the Kettle Black, the most feared
pirate frigate to ever sail the Seven
Seas...

'Excuse me,' said Mr Tiger. 'I don't
mean to stop you mid-sentence, but
do you think it would be less confusing
if you began by introducing Betsy K
Glory, instead of diving off the
deep end into the stormy sea
with the pirates? If I were
going to give a speech, I would
start by saying that Betsy has
purple hair, bright green eyes, rosy
cheeks and a sweet, freckly face.
And that she is the daughter of
Mr Alfonso Glory, who is known for
making the most amazing ice creams,
more delicious than any you have
ever tasted, on or off the map of the
world. Her mum is Myrtle, a mermaid

who doesn't have freckles and lives in the sea as mermaids do, whereas Dad and Betsy, who both have legs, live above Mr Glory's café in a tall, windy house. You could add, and it wouldn't be a whisker of a lie, that they are a very happy family. But then again, I'm not making a speech.'

'With great respect, Mr Tiger,' said the alphabet, 'we will tell this tale in our own way with our own words.'

'It's only a suggestion,' said Mr Tiger, 'but I'm fond of a good beginning and you need an exciting middle if all your words aren't going to fall flat in the end. Don't you agree?'

'Once upon a time...' said the letters of the alphabet.

'Purrfect!' said Mr Tiger.

3

·←· 2 ·→·

Betsy K Glory had felt sure that Mr Tiger would be back sooner than Sunday. But many Sundays had been and many Sundays had gone and the days began to feel as dull as a dog that hasn't been walked. Still there was neither whisker nor tail of Mr Tiger and his circus of Gongalong acrobats. Then, out of the blue, Betsy received a postcard. On the front was a drawing of a sea dragon. On the back, written in the unmistakable paw of Mr Tiger, it said: The tide is changing. There is a red rogue wind blowing.

Betsy didn't know what that meant.

She showed it to Dad, who was searching for his bicycle pump.

'What does this mean?' she asked.

'Search my socks,' he said.

Betsy picked up Dad's newspaper and read the headline:

AFTER FIFTY YEARS THE EGG
IS COMING HOME

She carried on reading while she ate her cornflakes:

We are delighted to announce that preparations are underway for the Festival of the Sea Dragon.

The article ended promising more exciting news soon.

To Betsy, the festival was the stuff of bedtime stories. There were not many islanders who could claim they'd ever been to one as they only happened every fifty years. The festival had two parts, the first was when a Pap-a-naggy came out of the sea carrying its egg.

You see, a sea dragon mother, a Mam-a-naggy, never leaves her sea apple orchard, seventy leagues below

the waves, and it is the Pap-a-naggy who, every fifty years, brings the egg to the island left off the map of the world. The islanders care for the egg and when the sea apples in the sea orchard have turned solid gold, the Pap-a-naggy knows that his egg has hatched and he returns for the second part of the festival. The islanders

dress in their best and there are street parties, and games, and a day of silliness and celebration. Everyone gathers to say a fond farewell to the baby sea dragon, the Nog-a-naggy, who returns with the Pap-a-naggy to the sea apple orchard and its mum.

'Crumble cakes!' said Betsy. 'And I'm going to see them now.'

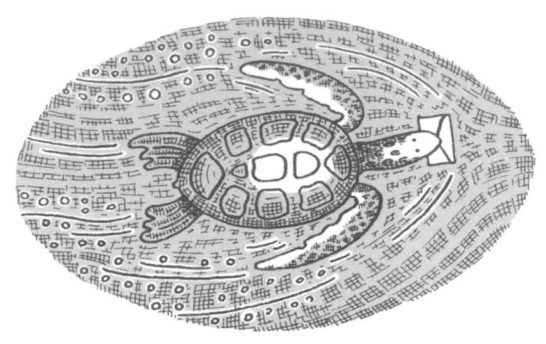

·← 3 →·

Next morning, which was Wednesday, Mum arrived with a letter that had been delivered by a turtle. It was from her sister, Betsy's Aunty Coral. Sitting in the kitchen with her tail in a bucket, Mum read aloud from the letter.

'Coral says she and the Siren Singers have been called away on siren duty.'

'Oh dear,' said Dad, alarmed.

'She goes on to say she would

have asked us to have Floss Grimm except that we don't have a mer-friendly house.'

'Not yet, my love,' said Dad.

'Who is Floss Grimm?' asked Betsy.

'Your cousin — remember?'

'Oh, yes, of course,' said Betsy, who, on account of having two legs and no tail, hadn't seen much of Mum's relatives.

'What is siren duty?'

Mum could be very watery when she wanted to be. She said it was to do with shipwrecks and pirates.

'Someone has to keep the seas clear of trouble and if we mermaids don't, who will?'

'How do you do it?' asked Betsy.

'Oh, by singing,' said Mum with a

faraway look in her eye, which meant
no further questions on the subject
would be answered.

'What else does the letter say?'

'That there have been several

sightings of pirate ships at the edge of the map of the world, and that Aunty Coral thinks it's a lot of seaweed over substance and that pirates never come this way.'

·←· 4 ·→·

Captain Calico Kettle was a roaring rage of a pirate. He had a blue beard, a wooden hand and three gold teeth. It was said that his temper was shorter than a gunpowder fuse, though he had somewhat mellowed these days. Now he wasn't so much looking for other ships to scupper as searching for the island that had been left off the map of the world. His quest had started when he'd heard an old smuggler's tale that had been passed from one

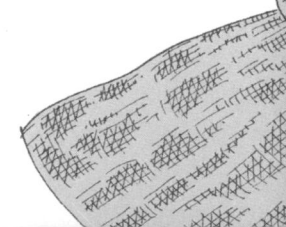

pirate's hairy face to another pirate's hairy ear. Like all stories that aren't written on paper, the tale had become as long as it was broad. But Captain Calico Kettle wanted the bare bones, with not a gram of a lie to fatten up the truth of it. And an old smuggler told him that he had proof that such an island did exist.

He'd whizzed and whirled his words into a sea fret until the captain snarled, 'Where's this proof? Show me the proof, you old bilge rat!' and the smuggler had brought out from his pantaloons a small chest that was chained to the wrist of what he called his wicked wooden hook.

'In here,' he said. 'In here is the proof.'

Captain Calico Kettle was not a patient man and with a single blow of his cutlass had taken the wicked wooden hook and the chest and skedaddled back to the Kettle Black.

There in his cabin he opened the chest, only to find a book full of pesky words that wouldn't stay still. He shouted at the scallywags, but it did no good. He called the bosun, the powder monkey and the cabin boy but none of them, or indeed any other member of his scurvy crew, could read the book either.

Captain Calico Kettle had an idea.

'We'll have to kidnap some landlubber who can read,' he said.

Three days later, through his spyglass he spotted a cruise liner. The captain of the cruise liner, seeing the Kettle Black, skull-and-crossbones flying, bearing down on him, made the sensible decision to abandon ship. He made sure all the passengers and crew escaped unharmed in the lifeboats.

All, that is, except Septimus Plank. Septimus was a handsome young man

who had trained to be a pastry chef and this was his first job, baking cakes and pastries for the passengers' tea. He had been so busy making cream puffs that he hadn't realised the cruise liner had been boarded by pirates. Septimus was extremely small and afterwards he thought that his lack of height might have been the reason he'd been overlooked by his crewmates.

Three-Legged Bill, the bosun of the Kettle Black, held poor Septimus upside down and shouted to Captain Calico Kettle.

'Shall I throw him overboard, Cap'n?'

'Yes,' said the captain. 'He's too puny to make a pirate.'

But just then a book fell out of Septimus's pocket.

'Hold hard there, Bill,' said Captain Calico Kettle. He picked up the book and opened it. Then he crouched and peered into Septimus's upside-down face. 'What's your name, lad?'

'S–Septimus Plank, sir.'

'Can you read all these pesky words that jump about as fast as fleas?'

'Y-yes, sir,' said Septimus. 'They are recipes. I'm a pastry chef.'

'Take him to the galley,' ordered the captain.

Pastry-making is not a skill that is in much demand when cooking for a whole load of greedy pirates, but what saved Septimus was the oldest trick in the book: he could read.

·← 5 →·

So it was that Septimus Plank found himself in the galley of the Kettle Black among the hens and the sacks of potatoes, doing his best to boil an egg for the captain's breakfast on a rolling sea with a storm brewing.

It should be said that for such a strong, burly man, Captain Calico Kettle was a very fussy eater. He would only eat a soft-boiled egg in the morning, with buttery, toasty soldiers to dip into it. His boiled egg had to be just right. It could not be too hard and it must not, on any account, ever be too runny. The trouble is that it's near impossible to boil an egg to perfection without the use of an egg-timer.

The minute Captain Calico Kettle saw Septimus carrying his breakfast tray, he snarled, showing his three gold teeth.

'It'd better be to my liking or else it will be the **PLANK** for you.'

He chuckled through his blue beard. He used his wooden hand to crack open the top of his egg. In went the spoon and out came the spoon. There was a moment's silence. Then he roared at Septimus in Tangerine, a language full of juicy words that

only the nastiest pirates understand, although Septimus got the zest of what he was saying.

'It would help,' said Septimus, 'if I had an egg-timer.'

'An egg-timer? What is an egg-timer?' asked the captain.

Septimus tried to explain but Captain Calico Kettle raised his

wooden hand to silence him. Etched on his palm were the words, **BE QUIET OR ELSE.** The 'ELSE' was hard to read, although the meaning of the hand gesture was clear to everyone.

'You're no good at boiling eggs,' he yelled. 'But if you can read this—' The captain picked up an old, dog-eared book that was lying beside the unloved egg. 'Then I won't have you thrown to the sharks.'

Septimus read the book. It told of an island left off the map of the world, of sea dragons and mermaids. But the part that Captain Calico Kettle was most interested in was about a sea orchard and its golden apples.

'The orchard is seventy leagues beneath the waves, Captain,' said

Septimus. 'SEVENTY leagues,' he repeated.

'Don't be a limp gumpit — no orchard grows below the waves,' bellowed the captain. 'It's those pesky words, they're jiggling about to hide the truth. Read it again. Where is the island to be found, Septimus Plank?'

'The book says that on a moonless night, a red rogue wind rises between sea areas Fair Codsroes and Biscuit.'

'Then what? Go on, go on...'

'Then you have to find the storm — and sail into the red rogue wind.'

·✦ 6 ✦·

While everyone on the island was busy getting ready for the arrival of the Pap-a-naggy, Princess Albee sailed in on her yacht for the festival. She had lived here for a spell as a toad and had grown fond of the place. Now the spell had been broken and she was a princess again. She considered the island left off the map of the world her second home. She also wanted to say a proper thank you to Dad, Mum

and Betsy, for without their help, and
that of Mr Tiger and the Gongalong
acrobats, the moon might never have
turned blue. Then Mr Glory could
not have made the Gongalong-berry
wishable ice cream that broke the

spell she'd been under. And she would still have been a toad with a very long tongue.

Betsy had seen the boat in the distance from her bedroom window and hoped it might be Mr Tiger. She was a bit disappointed it wasn't. Still, it was good to see Princess Albee again. Dad made special ice cream in honour of her visit. He called it, 'Princess Pineapple Mango Delight'.

'Delicious,' said Princess Albee, spooning the ice cream out of the tall glass. 'This ice cream tastes of happy-ever-afters, rather than wishes.'

Mum swished her tail in the bucket of water and asked Princess Albee if she had found her happy-ever-after.

'Yes,' said Princess Albee.

'Have you met a prince?' asked Betsy.

'You don't need a prince for a happy-ever-after,' said Mum.

'And it's far harder than you think to meet the right prince,' said Princess Albee. 'Most are frogs, and no amount of magic will change that.'

'That's a pity,' said Betsy, who liked the idea of being invited to a royal wedding.

'It's not important,' said Princess Albee to Betsy. 'I'm very happy in my own ever-after.'

She wanted to know how Mum managed. 'I mean, houses aren't exactly designed for mermaids.'

'We get along swimmingly,' said Mum.

'I live in the sea. Alfonso and Betsy live above the café.'

Before Princess Albee left, she presented the Glorys with three gifts. For Dad, there was a French horn, for Mum, bright pink knitting needles, and for Betsy, a tiny gold seahorse on a chain to wear round her neck.

All too soon the sun rolled out of the hot lazy sky down into the sea for a quick dip before it retired for the night.

And Betsy, tucked up in her bed, said dreamily to herself, 'Maybe tomorrow, Mr Tiger will be here.'

· ← 7 →·

Thursday — being the day that follows Wednesday, whether it wants to or not — arrived, and into the harbour sailed Mr Tiger's blue-and-white-striped ship. Mr Tiger stood at the prow waving, and as soon as the gangplank was lowered, Betsy ran up it to greet him. Mr Tiger lifted her off her feet.

'I've missed you, Mr Tiger,' she said.

'And I have missed you, Betsy K

Glory,' said Mr Tiger. 'Did you receive my postcard?'

'Yes, I did. But what does it mean?'

'That is an excellent question.'

Betsy took his paw and led him to the tall windy house.

Dad had moved a bathtub into the

café and Mum sat there knitting with her bright pink knitting needles.

Mr Tiger purred. 'A gift from Princess Albee, I take it.'

'Yes,' said Mum, carefully picking up a stitch she'd dropped.

Betsy hadn't a clue why Princess Albee thought Mum might want to knit. She was not a knitting kind of mum.

'Have you ever knitted before?' Betsy asked.

'No,' said Mum. 'I haven't had the right type of needles before.'

'Princess Albee gave Dad a French horn,' said Betsy to Mr Tiger, 'which will be useful on his bicycle rounds. And she gave me a gold seahorse — look.'

'A very magical gift indeed,' said Mr Tiger.

'How is it magical?'

Mr Tiger blinked his golden eyes.

'If you're not going to tell me why my seahorse is magical, perhaps you will tell me what your postcard meant now. What is the red rogue wind?'

Mr Tiger snarled. 'Trouble,' he said darkly. 'And that's one thing we do not need the day before the Pap-a-naggy is due to arrive.'

·← 8 →·

When Mr Tiger came to Mr Glory's café on the morning of the great day, he had an air of mystery about him. Betsy had a feeling he was up to something, but what? Dad was about to put Mum in the bathtub when Mr Tiger let out a low growl.

'I have brought a present for Myrtle,' he said, and threw open the door.

Two Gongalongs tumbled in carrying a most oddly-shaped package.

'I was thinking,' said Mr Tiger, 'that when a mermaid tries to live on land she has to rely on others to ferry her about.'

'I don't mind,' said Dad. 'Truly, I don't.'

'But I do,' said Mum. 'I like the water as there I'm free. Here, my dear Alfonso, you have to do so much for me.'

Dad looked sad.

'Cheer up, Alfonso,' said Mr Tiger, patting Dad on the back. 'Unwrap the present for your mum, Betsy.'

Betsy did and there stood the most extraordinary contraption. It was a sit-up tin bath on wheels with pedals to turn with your hands. It had been painted to look like a mermaid's tail and was full of salt water. Mum was

speechless, so was Dad. Then she
burst out laughing.

'Of course,' said Mr Tiger, 'if you
don't like the colour it could always
be changed.'

'No, no,' said Mum. 'This is just
what we need.'

As soon as Dad lifted her into the
sit-up tin bath she set off out of the
café for the harbour. She whizzed

this way and that way, with Betsy running behind her giggling.

'Oh, Mr Tiger,' said Mum when she returned. 'This is ideal. Thank you so much.'

'Now tell me,' said Mr Tiger. 'Have we enough ice cream for the day?'

'Yes,' said Betsy and she called out all the ice cream names. 'We have Raspberry Ribble Wonder, Chocolate Toffee Delight, Lemon Sugar Shocker, Strawberry Sparklers, Popping Peanut Plenties, Myrtle's Minty Mumbo Marvel, Chocolate Cherry Delight and Knickerbocker...'

'But wait,' said Mr Tiger. 'Haven't we forgotten the Pap-a-naggy's special ice cream?'

'No,' said Dad. And he showed Mr Tiger five buckets filled with an ice cream called Salty Sweet Seaweed. 'It's made to a secret recipe handed down by my late grandfather. He made it the last time the sea dragon visited fifty years ago. He told me it was the sea dragon's favourite flavour so far.'

'Then everything is ship-shape,' said Mr Tiger.

☆ ☆

That afternoon, Princess Albee joined Mr Tiger on a specially-built platform by the harbour wall and everybody gathered together. All they had to do was wait until the great bell on the bell tower in the market place struck two o'clock. Mr Tiger, being a ringmaster, was put in charge of the ceremony and at a sign from him Alfonso Glory blew his French horn. A fountain of water rose into the sky, the sea began to foam and from it reared the head of the sea dragon followed by his scaly body. It was a terrifying sight, for he was far more majestic than anyone had imagined.

With great delicacy the Pap-a-naggy squeezed past Mr Tiger's blue-and-white-striped ship and Princess

Albee's yacht until he stood near the
harbour wall.

There was an awkward silence.
The kind of silence there is when you

meet an ancient aunt and don't know
what to say.

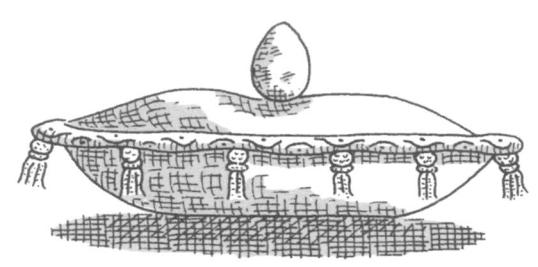

᛫ᚴ 9 ᚴ᛫

Mr Tiger stepped forward to address the Pap-a-naggy with Betsy holding tight to his paw.

'On behalf of the people of the island left off the map of the world, I welcome you, the great Pap-a-naggy, to our shores,' he said. 'We are honoured that you have chosen us to look after your egg until it hatches. We will not let you down. We have never let you down. I am certain that this little sea dragon will be the golden apple of his parents' eyes. I, my gutsy Gongalongs, Princess Albee and all our island friends will remember this day for ever.'

The Gongalongs threw their pointy hats into the air and the islanders cheered. 'Hip hip hurray!'

The sea dragon didn't seem to be carrying anything. Betsy wondered if he might have forgotten the egg, for, like everyone else, she imagined a sea dragon's egg would be huge.

When the Pap-a-naggy opened his scaly talon there lay an egg no bigger than a hen's egg. The Pap-a-naggy seemed reluctant to place it on the golden cushion that the mayor held in his very shaky hands. Mr Tiger gave Betsy a little nudge. She took the cushion from the mayor and bravely

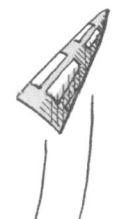

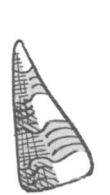
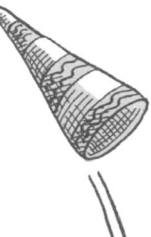
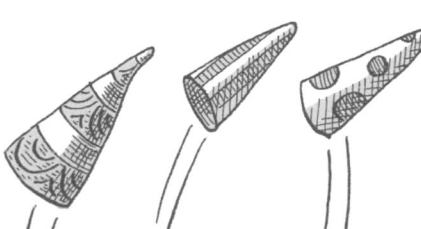

held it as still as still could be. Then the Pap-a-naggy put his egg on it and opened his other scaly talon to reveal a garland of silver apple blossom that he solemnly presented to Princess Albee. As he watched Betsy carry the egg to the town hall, accompanied by the town's brass band, the Pap-a-naggy let out the most terrible wail. Betsy was back at the harbour before you could say 'shimmering shrimps'.

'I think he's crying,' said Betsy.

'Yes,' said Mum. 'It's hard to leave someone you love.'

'Perhaps he shouldn't leave it,' said Betsy. 'Perhaps he should keep the little egg with him.'

'Unfortunately,' said Mum, 'that

would be the end of the egg, as they must hatch on land if they are ever going to survive in the sea.'

'Crumble cakes,' said Betsy.

Mum sighed. 'Many things are the opposite of what they should be,' she said.

Dad, meanwhile, had put all five buckets of the Salty Sweet Seaweed ice cream into a wheelbarrow and pushed it as close to the sea dragon as he dared.

First the Pap-a-naggy snitted it, then he put one of his talons in the bucket and licked it for a rather long time.

Suddenly, he went from being an unhappy sea dragon to a delighted sea dragon and he began to speak in a language that only Mum understood.

'He's speaking Tangerine,' whispered Mum to Dad and Betsy. 'It's a language spoken mainly by sailors, but there are a few of us in the ocean who understand it.' She began to translate. 'He is saying that... he has never tasted ice cream as wickedly wonderful as this... and that —' Mum laughed — 'that the ice cream he had last time he was here tasted disgusting... far too salty! This, on the other talon, is perfection.'

Mum continued to giggle while Dad gave a little bow and said thank you to the Pap-a-naggy.

After the last morsel was gone and

he had licked
the buckets
clean, the
Pap-a-naggy
— to everyone's
amazement —
lifted Dad off his
feet. Before you could
say 'sizzling sugar' he had given Dad
a hug and put him back on the ground.

The islanders cheered and the
brass band played, the mighty Pap-
a-naggy turned, swam out of the
harbour and, whistling a sea shanty,
disappeared under the waves.

·← 10 →·

Captain Calico Kettle found the red rogue wind exactly where the smuggler's book said he would and told his crew to sail straight into it.

'This, my hearties,' he said, 'will be a storm to remember.'

The red rogue wind began to puff its cheeks in fury, rain danced shiny over the decks of the Kettle Black and the further into the storm the ship sailed, the more the red rogue wind raged until waves rose to the size of mountains. The gale turned sails to rags and snapped masts, tearing the rigging into spider webs. Thunder roared and rattled, lightning flashed across the elephant-grey sky.

The pirates on the Kettle Black clung on for dear life. Captain Calico Kettle ordered everything but essentials to be thrown overboard. Barrels, cannonballs, sacks of potatoes, all went into the sea, and Septimus was expecting that he and the hens would be next when a gust of wind blew the ship into a wall of water. It swept the boat up and

brought it crashing down again. All on board were certain they had hit the rocks and, just when they feared the ship was lost, they found themselves in a kipper-calm sea beneath a picture book blue sky. It was quiet except for the call of the seagulls.

'I think,' said Captain Calico Kettle, as he looked through his spyglass, 'we be in uncharted waters.'

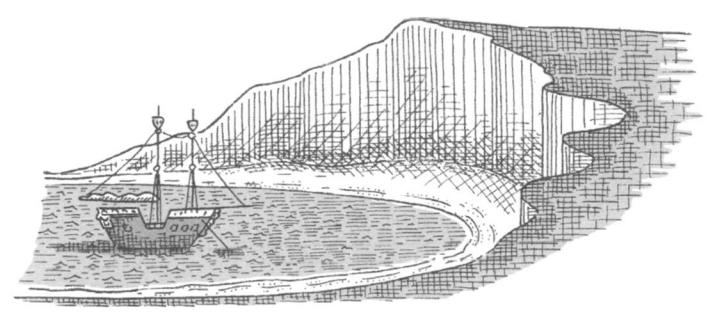

·← 11 →·

The Kettle Black anchored in a cove on the island left off the map of the world.

'All we need to do now,' said Captain Calico Kettle, 'is find the golden apple orchard then we will be as rich as Croesus.'

'That must be very rich,' said Three-Legged Bill, the bosun. 'There are more creases in the world than anyone can ever iron out.'

But Captain Calico Kettle had a

problem. He needed to know where on the island the golden apple orchard grew, and he couldn't very well ask an islander. He would be spotted as a pirate straightaway.

'Let's send the powder monkey,' said Three-Legged Bill. 'He's a useless powder monkey but he speaks nicely and scrubs up well.'

The powder monkey was not pleased at being ordered to wash the gunpowder off his face and hands and smarten himself up. But when he realised his mission was to explore the island and make a map of where the golden apple orchard could be found, he cheered up. The bosun rowed him ashore and watched as the lad set off up the cliff with his notebook and pencil.

All day the captain and crew of the Kettle Black waited for the powder monkey to come back. Captain Calico Kettle's fuse became shorter and shorter and by the time the powder monkey returned to the ship, night had fallen and the captain's fuse was about to blow.

The poor lad had hardly climbed aboard before the captain seized him by the collar of his unusually clean shirt.

'Did you find it? Did you find the golden apple orchard? Where is it?'

'Here's the thing, Captain,' said the powder monkey. 'The orchard isn't

actually on the land but under the sea.'

Captain Calico Kettle shook the powder monkey as if to rattle the truth out of him. But the powder monkey had something else to say.

'There's another thing, Captain. The islanders are looking after an egg.'

'An egg? What sort of egg?'

'I don't know, it looked like an ordinary sort of egg such as you have for your breakfast, Captain. But the thing is...'

'What is this thing? Come to the point, before I...'

'They look after the egg until it hatches and they are rewarded with a golden apple.'

'HA!' said the captain.

He called the crew together and bellowed at them in Tangerine.

'I've fought the red rogue wind and I will not leave empty-handed. What is our motto? What is our motto, me hearties?'

'Treasure keeps us together,' sang the crew. 'No matter whatever, treasure keeps us together.'

'I have a plan,' said Captain Calico Kettle. 'A wicked plan. I'm going ashore. Septimus Plank — bring me a hen's egg.'

·← 12 →·

Septimus's only friends aboard the Kettle Black were the hens. They had been a sad and scraggy bunch. The old cockerel had lost the spring in his step, the hens were scrawny and suffered from seasickness. Septimus had gone to a lot of effort to make things better for them. The hens had rewarded him by laying beautiful eggs.

He chose the largest egg he could find. It was still warm as he put it in a woolly sock for safekeeping then went to the captain's cabin.

'And another thing,' the powder monkey was saying, 'is the ice cream.'

Septimus expected Captain Calico Kettle to bellow that ice cream didn't interest him, but a soft expression settled on his face.

'I love ice cream,' he said. 'I haven't had proper ice cream since my mum made it for me when I was a tiddler.'

Septimus knew this was a short-lived lull before the wind of the captain's temper changed. Change it did, and he booted the powder monkey out of his cabin.

'What's that?' said Captain Calico Kettle, pointing to Septimus's sock.

'It's the egg you asked for, sir.'

Septimus explained that the egg would have to be handled with care and perhaps it would be a good idea if he went with the captain to make sure it didn't break.

'You think the cap'n was born this side of Sunday?' said Three-Legged Bill.

The crew laughed heartily and Captain Calico Kettle held up his wooden hand. Everyone fell silent except for the gulls.

'You're fond of the hens, aren't you?' the captain said to Septimus.

'They're family to me,' said Septimus.

The captain looked long and hard at Septimus Plank. Captain Calico Kettle had to admit that if his one and only good hand was holding the egg, it would be tricky to hold his cutlass as well. And then how would he ward off an attack?

After about three seconds he agreed that Septimus should come with him. But if he tried any funny stuff, the hens would be made to walk the plank.

The sun had set rose petal red and the sky was pulling its midnight-blue velvet cloth over the day.

Just as the lights went out in the
town and all the islanders had fallen
fast asleep, Captain Calico Kettle
and the pastry chef arrived on shore.

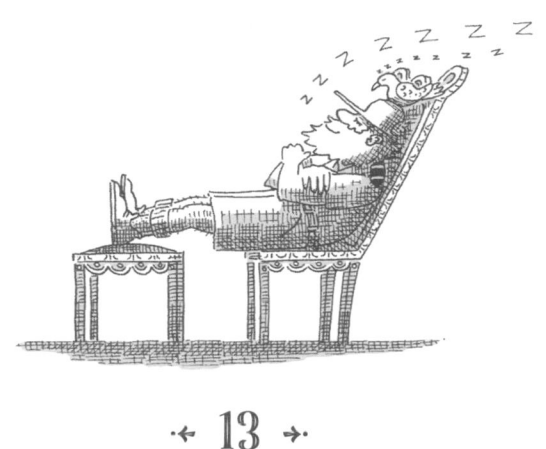

·+ 13 +·

That night it was the turn of the harbour-master to guard the egg. He was so sure that everything was fine and dandy that he had fallen asleep. After all, nothing bad ever happened on the island that had been left off the map of the world. None of the islanders ever locked their doors or windows. Nothing had ever been stolen. The harbour-master was soon dreaming of ships with golden sails.

Captain Calico Kettle ordered
Septimus Plank to take off his shoes.

'My tiptoeing days are over,' said
the captain. 'Now, lad, you know what
to do. And remember, no hanky-panky
or those hens walk the plank.'

Septimus tiptoed up the steps to
the town hall and was surprised to find

the doors unlocked, and even more surprised to discover in the middle of the marble foyer a man asleep in a chair beside the egg. It was dark and it took a while for Septimus to realise that next to the egg was an egg-timer. Carefully, he took the hen's egg out of his sock and swapped it with the egg on the golden cushion. He wondered why anyone would be guarding an egg. That was odd. But the egg-timer would be jolly useful. He slipped it into his pocket and crept towards the door. He was about to leave when the lights on a yacht in the harbour lit up and there on the deck stood a young woman. She was as pretty as a picture and as delicate as a china cup. Septimus's heart gave a leap.

'Come on,' hissed Captain Calico Kettle, who was waiting at the foot of the steps.

They had quite a way to walk back to the rowing boat that was waiting in the cove. All Septimus could think about was the lovely creature he had seen on the yacht. As the oars skimmed the water he wished upon a star that he might one day have a chance to meet her.

Captain Calico Kettle was very pleased with the night's work.

'They will only have the egg back if they give me a crate — no, two crates — no, make that three crates — of golden apples.'

·← 14 →·

As nothing had ever been stolen before on the island left off the map of the world, it never crossed the harbour-master's mind, or anyone else's, that it was strange that the egg-timer had disappeared. Everybody bent over backwards to say that perhaps it had been forgotten, or that it had never been there in the first place. And, of course, it didn't occur to the harbour-master that anything had happened to the sea dragon's egg, for the hen's egg was much the same size and colour.

Mr Tiger had known something was wrong the moment he'd woken up for his tail twitched and his whiskers niggled him.

'Egg-timers don't go missing,' he growled to himself as he ate his breakfast at Mr Glory's café.

His pocket-watch was of no use. The red rogue wind was playing havoc with its tick-tock timings. Perhaps, he thought, Betsy might have heard or seen something unusual. He was

about to ask when he was distracted
by Mum's clicking knitting, which
often ties tigers' thoughts in tangles.

She cast off the final stitch.

'Put this on, Betsy,' she said.

Betsy did. Whatever it was
supposed to be, it looked a mess. It
was far too long, it was incredibly
itchy, it went over her head and her
face and she couldn't see where
she was going. Worse still,
she couldn't hear a word
of what was being said.
Everyone sounded as if

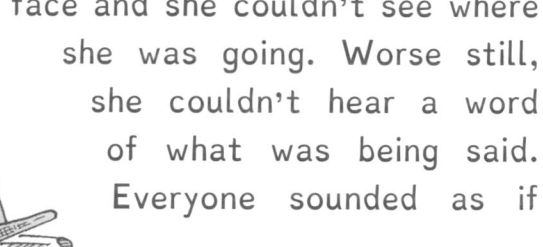

they were talking underwater. Betsy pulled down the headpiece.

'Mum,' she said. 'This doesn't fit.'

'It's not meant to. Not yet,' said Mum.

'It looks perfectly well made,' Mr Tiger purred. 'I can't see any dropped stitches.'

'There are none,' said Mum. 'I made sure there were no holes.'

Not even Dad said a word about the garment not fitting or looking stupid.

'Well,' he said, 'I suppose we'd better get on with it.'

'On with what?' asked Betsy. 'You don't mean I have to go out in this?'

Dad nodded.

Betsy had no idea why

anyone thought this was a good plan.
Everyone would laugh at her.

Mr Tiger picked up his walking
stick, Dad sat Betsy on the edge
of Mum's tin bath and they made
a strange little procession as they
went down to the quayside.

First, Dad helped Mum into the
sea and then lifted Betsy off the tin
bath.

'Wait a minute,' said Betsy. 'If
I go in the water wearing this, I'll
drown.'

'No, you won't,' said Mum. 'Pull it up — right over your head.'

Betsy was about to say a whole load of Buts when she found herself being handed down to Mum and disappearing under the water.

Then something happened.

Something that Betsy couldn't ever have imagined happening. The knitted garment that had been itchy and scratchy and too big began to shrink until it fitted her like skin.

All the stitches became
translucent and looking down
she realised that her legs were
encased in a mermaid's tail.

Mum beamed.

'You see?' she said. 'I was just
waiting for the right knitting needles.'

Usually when Betsy was underwater
everything sounded strange and
bubbly. Now it was tin-can clear.
Her vision underwater was as crystal
sharp as if she was on land.

'Oh, crumble cakes,' said Betsy.
'This is fantastic, Mum!'

It took Betsy a little time to swim
like a mermaid and get used to the
fact she didn't have to go up for air.

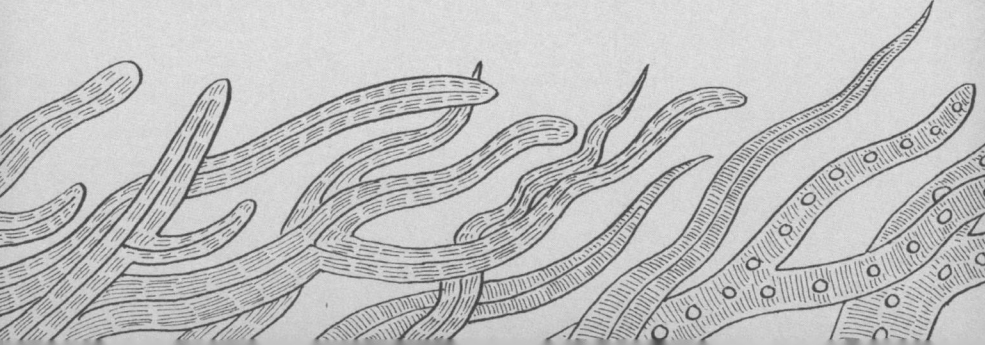

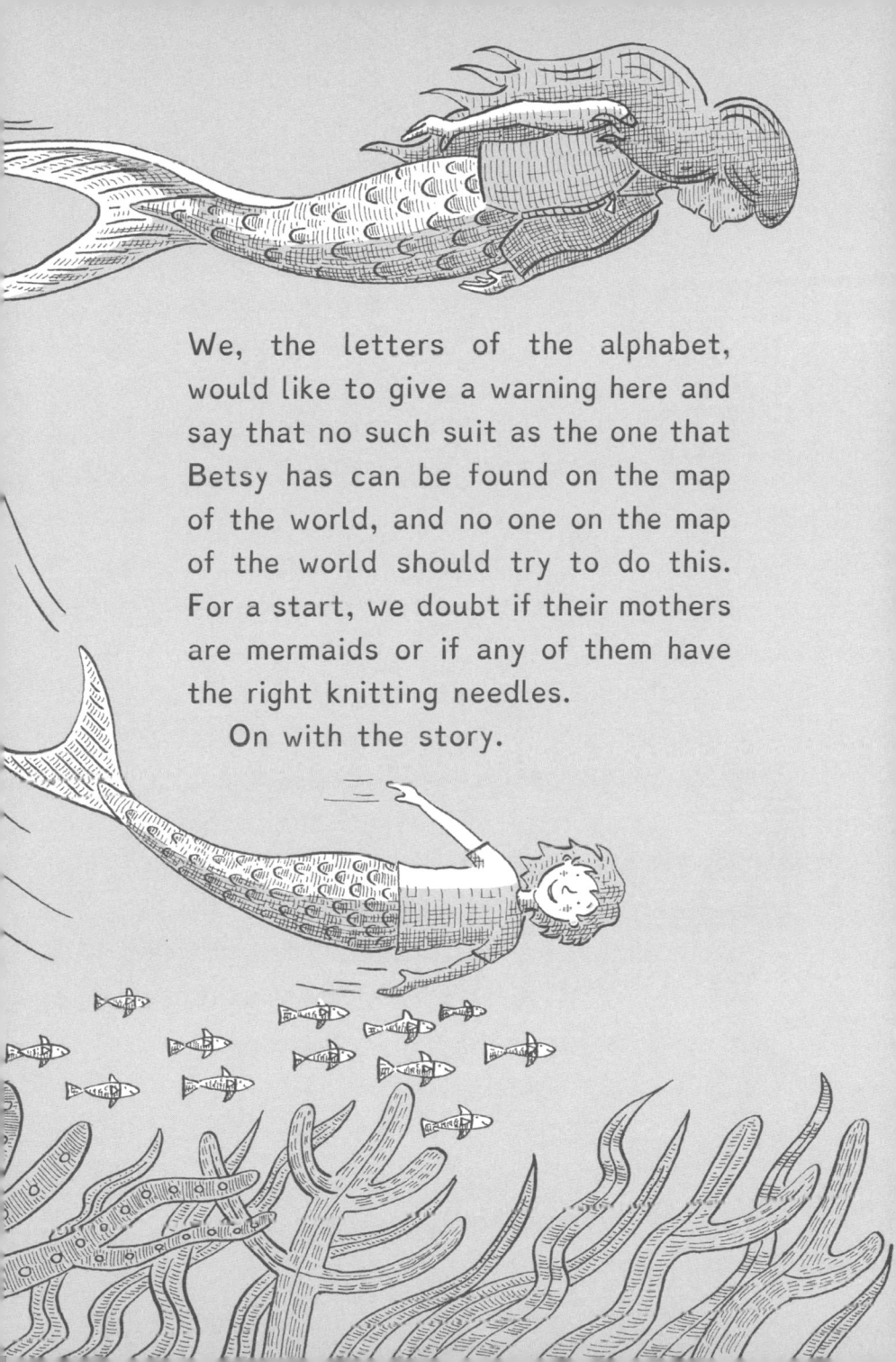

We, the letters of the alphabet, would like to give a warning here and say that no such suit as the one that Betsy has can be found on the map of the world, and no one on the map of the world should try to do this. For a start, we doubt if their mothers are mermaids or if any of them have the right knitting needles.

On with the story.

Being underwater and not having to worry about goggles or breathing meant there was a whole glorious world that Betsy had never noticed before. The shells glimmered, the fish shimmered and everyone knew Mum, even the shrimps.

'Is that your daughter?' said a seahorse. 'Well, I never — she looks just like you.'

A dozing octopus woke and waved its tentacles as they swam past.

'Oh, Myrtle, what a suit you have knitted. Will the dear darling be living here with us now?'

'No,' said Mum.

'Good to see you both,' said a turtle. 'Have you heard the news?'

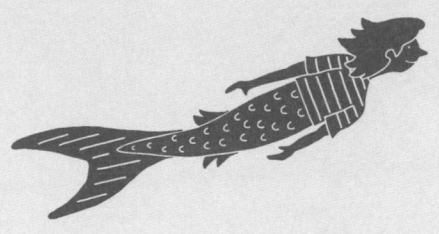

'What news?' said Mum.

'The news swimming towards you,' said the turtle.

And that was when they saw him: a merboy with bright blue hair.

'Aunty Myrtle,' he called. 'It's Floss — Floss Grimm, your nephew.'

'I know perfectly well who you are,' said Mum. 'What I don't know is what you're doing here.'

Floss Grimm didn't reply. He was staring at his cousin.

'Wow, Betsy — I've never seen a suit like that. You look terrific — you swim just like a mermaid.'

·←· **15** ·→·

Dad and Mr Tiger were very surprised when they went to help Mum and Betsy out of the sea to find Floss Grimm with them.

'Hi, Uncle Alfonso,' said Floss Grimm.

Betsy noticed that he said it in a way that sounded as if he had been expected at the café all along. Dad picked him up. It was only when they got back to the café and Betsy had taken off her suit and carefully hung it up that she realised how much trouble Floss Grimm was in. Mum said that her sister Coral, Floss Grimm's mum, would be furious when she found out that Floss was not at Dolphin Summer School.

Floss explained that he had had quite enough of Dolphin School as it was very serious and the dolphins didn't play games, the food was horrible and they never ever had ice cream.

That made Mum laugh.

'Please don't send me back,' said Floss.

'For the time being,' said Mum, 'you are our guest.'

Dad brought Floss a bucket of water.

That night they were invited to supper on Mr Tiger's blue-and-white-striped ship, where Mum and

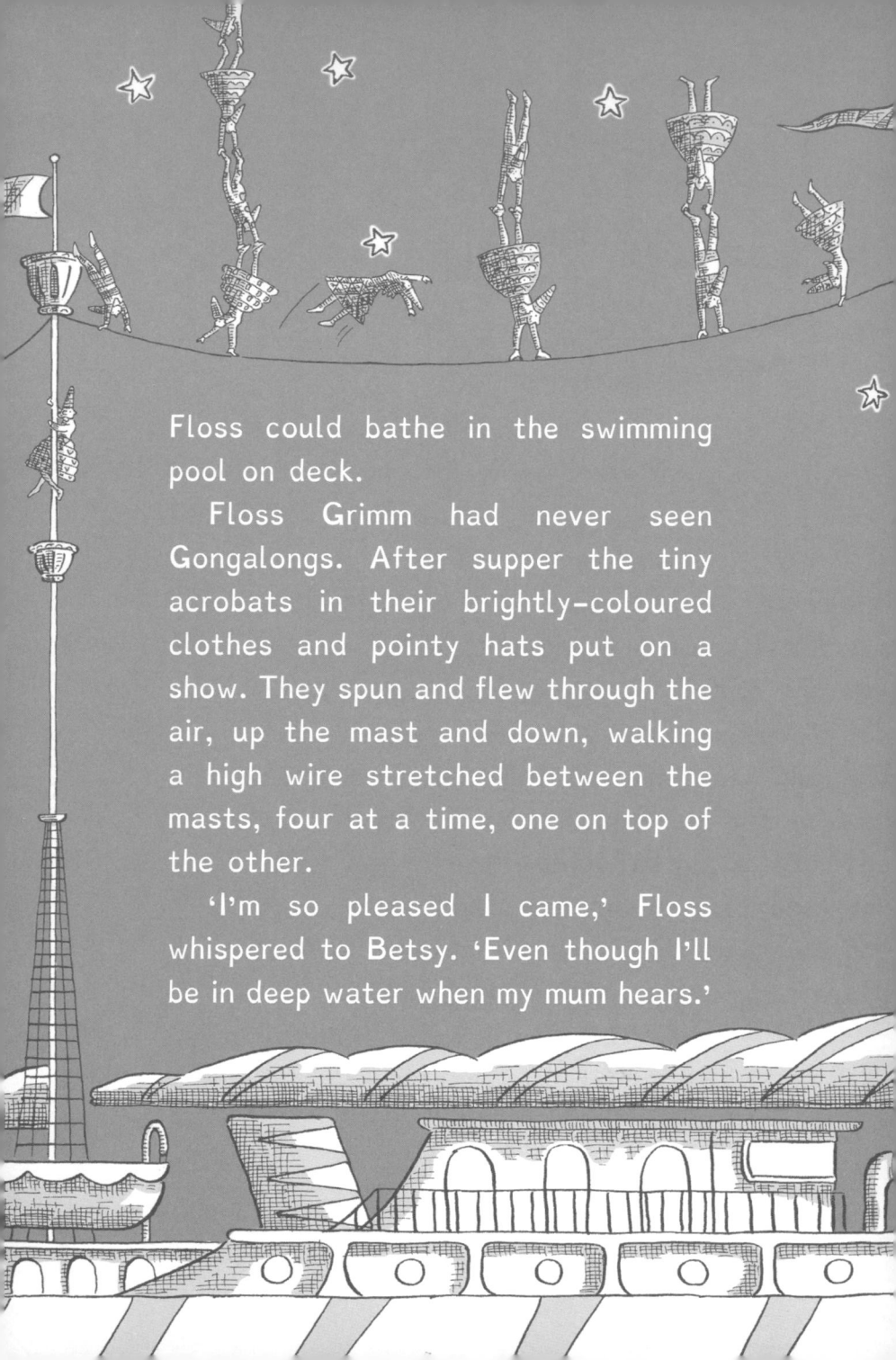

Floss could bathe in the swimming pool on deck.

Floss Grimm had never seen Gongalongs. After supper the tiny acrobats in their brightly-coloured clothes and pointy hats put on a show. They spun and flew through the air, up the mast and down, walking a high wire stretched between the masts, four at a time, one on top of the other.

'I'm so pleased I came,' Floss whispered to Betsy. 'Even though I'll be in deep water when my mum hears.'

Betsy was
so busy talking to
Floss that she didn't notice Mr Tiger
studying his pocket-watch. He had
seen in its glass a misty image of
a skull-and-crossbones flag flying,
which could only mean one thing. She
heard him growl.

'What is it?' she asked, turning to
look at him.

'Pirates,' said Mr Tiger. 'Pesky
pirates.'

·← 16 →·

On the Kettle Black the pirates were busy repairing the storm damage. Septimus, thanks to the egg-timer, had for the first time cooked a perfect egg for the captain's breakfast.

Captain Calico Kettle was in a good mood — if such a hard-boiled pirate could ever be in a good mood.

'Where's the other egg?' he asked.

'I have it safe in my sock, in my pocket, sir,' said Septimus.

The captain held out his one good hand.

Septimus didn't want to let the egg go. He felt connected to it. He had never felt like this about an egg before.

He took the egg out of his sock and they both stared at it. There was no doubt — the egg had grown. It was bigger than a goose's egg. No one could possibly mistake it for a hen's egg.

'It's grown overnight, sir,' said Septimus.

The captain bellowed for the powder monkey.

'Did you tell me everything you heard on the island? Think, lad, think hard. Was there anything else?'

The powder monkey screwed up his face. 'Well, Captain, there was another thing, actually.'

'What thing — actually?'

'A sort of festival thing. It's called the Festival of the Sea Dragon.'

'Why didn't you say that before, you warbling weevil-eater?' said the captain and threw the powder monkey out of his cabin.

'I think, Septimus Plank, that we might have hit the bull's-eye. I think this be a sea dragon's egg.'

Captain Calico Kettle danced a jig on the spot.

'Now, lad, you're going to write a letter addressed to the big-wig of the island and say if they want the sea dragon's egg back then they must send me a crate of golden apples. No, make that two. But then again, two is not a number I am that fond of, so make it three crates of golden apples.'

Septimus began to write.

Dear Sir,

Help. My name is Septimus Plank. I am not a pirate. I have been kidnapped. I have the sea dragon's egg safe in my sock. Please rescue my hens and me. The Kettle Black can be found if you turn left out of the town and then go straight on until you come to the cliff then turn right towards the sea and it's in the cove.

Thank you in advance.

Yours faithfully,

S Plank (pastry chef)

The captain counted the words.

'There are more of them than I thought would be needed,' he said.

'This one —' he pointed to the word 'Help' — 'what is it? I'm sure I know it.'

'Hen,' said Septimus weakly. 'I may not be able to read,' said Captain Calico Kettle, 'but I know when an egg-boiler is trying to scuttle my plans.' He screwed up Septimus's letter. 'Do you think I'm a ship's biscuit short of a tin? You'll never hornswoggle me, my lad. I'm not called Captain Calico Kettle for nothing. You and your hens will walk the plank...'

'But, Captain...'

Captain Calico Kettle held up his hand. 'You will walk the plank tomorrow morning — just as soon as you've boiled my breakfast egg.'

·← 17 →·

The following morning, Mr Tiger had his breakfast egg at Mr Glory's café with Princess Albee. The princess thought that as it was such a lovely day, she might go for a ride. Her yacht had stabling on board and she had brought her little white pony with her.

'I'll be back in time for an ice cream tea,' she said.

Mr Tiger's tail twitched and his whiskers niggled him — he felt something was wrong. But he didn't want to worry the princess. He took out his pocket-watch and still he could not make stripes nor dots of it. It showed a picture of a chicken. He'd decided he should ask the harbour-master some questions about the missing egg-timer when Dad came downstairs carrying Floss Grimm, who'd spent the night in the bathroom. Betsy slid down the banister, carrying her mermaid suit, and, as usual, landed in a heap at the bottom of the stairs.

'Can I go for a swim with Floss, Dad?' she called.

Dad was helping Floss into the old pram that he had spent most of the night making watertight so Floss could be pushed about in it on land.

Just then, the bells in the tower in the market place began to ring. It was the sort of ring that only happened in an emergency.

Mr Tiger, Betsy and Dad rushed to see what was going on. Unfortunately, Dad forgot to put the brake on the pram, which rolled gently down to the quayside and stopped with a bump, tipping Floss over the harbour wall.

When Dad caught up with the pram, Floss was in the sea.

'Don't worry, Uncle Alfonso, I wanted a morning swim.'

'I can go with him, Dad, can't I?' asked Betsy.

Dad was all in a fluster and said, 'Yes.' No sooner was the word out

of his mouth
than she had
slipped into her
mermaid suit and disappeared into the
sea. Dad didn't have time to worry
because Mrs Rose, the lady from the
flower shop, came running from the
town hall.

'It's a chicken! It's a chicken,' she
shouted. 'The sea dragon's egg has
hatched, and it's a chicken!'

Mr Tiger strode into the town hall
and there, on the golden cushion,
surrounded by broken eggshell, sat a
fluffy yellow chick.

'That is definitely not a sea dragon,'
said Mr Tiger.

The mayor, still in his pyjamas,

came downstairs from his flat to see what the fuss was about.

'Oh, no,' he said. 'Oh, no, no, no. This is a calamity. What could possibly have gone wrong? Do you think the sea dragon made a mistake? What are we going to tell him when he comes to collect his baby? We can't present him with a chick. No, no, no. I will have to resign.'

'Something rotten is going on,' said Mr Tiger. 'Fortunately, Mr Mayor, I have aboard my ship a hot-air balloon. I think now might be the time to take it out for an airing.'

Mum had come from the café in her contraption and found Dad at the town-hall steps.

'Where are Betsy and Floss?' she asked.

'Oh, they went for a swim. But, Myrtle, the sea dragon egg has hatched and it's a chicken.'

'No,' said Mum. 'That's impossible.'

'Unless,' said Mr Tiger as he joined them, 'the egg has been poached.'

'Poached?' said Dad.

'Yes, poached — stolen — by someone who has been on the island and shouldn't have been. I intend to find out who it was.'

'Alfonso,' said Mum, 'help me into the sea. Someone must keep an eye on Betsy and Floss Grimm. You go with Mr Tiger.' And she vanished beneath the waves.

'Come along, Alfonso,' said Mr Tiger. 'There's not a moment to lose.'

'Oh dear,' said Dad, as the Gongalongs inflated the hot-air balloon. 'I don't like heights.'

'I feel much the same about pirates,' said Mr Tiger.

'Pirates?' said Dad. 'They never come this way.'

Septimus had been allowed to cook supper the night before, which the pirates thought was rather good. While he was preparing the meal, the sea dragon's egg started to hatch. Septimus couldn't believe his eyes. By the time he'd finished serving the lemon meringue pie, standing on the worktop in the galley was the sweetest little sea dragon you have ever seen. Not that Septimus had ever seen a sea dragon before, sweet or otherwise. He put out his hand, and the little sea dragon jumped on to it and, taking the pastry chef's sleeve in his tiny claws, began to suck it. Oh dear, thought Septimus. What should I feed it on? He wondered if it would like a few crumbs of pastry. But it was at this moment that Three-Legged Bill came to take Septimus to the hold. Septimus quickly took off his pastry chef's hat and put it over the baby sea dragon to hide it.

'And then it's the plank for you in the morning, lad,' said the bosun. 'Soon as the cap'n's had his egg.'

'Surely it would be best if I washed up,' said Septimus, 'before you take me to the hold?'

As no pirate likes washing up, Septimus was given another fifteen minutes of freedom. When he'd

finished, he put the largest of the hens' eggs in the sock while trying to explain to the hens and the baby sea dragon that tomorrow he had to walk the plank and that he wouldn't see them again because he couldn't swim.

And this is the strangest bit: the hens and the baby sea dragon seemed to get the drift of what was going to happen.

Septimus spent the night in the hold and next morning boiled his last egg for Captain Calico Kettle with the baby sea dragon perched on his head, out of sight under his pastry chef's hat. For some reason he didn't understand, he popped the egg-timer into his pocket.

When the time came, the hens and the cockerel followed him up

on deck. Septimus was blindfolded
and his hands tied behind his back.
It became clear that Captain Calico
Kettle expected the hens to walk the
plank, and Three-Legged Bill, with
much sighing and grumbling, had to
blindfold them too.

'Wait!' shouted the captain.
'Where is the sock with the sea
dragon's egg in it?'

'In the galley, Cap'n,' said the bosun and sent a deck-hand to fetch it.

Septimus was at the very end of the plank when Captain Calico Kettle let out a terrible cry.

'This is the **WRONG EGG** — come back here, you landlubbing louse.'

Septimus did the only thing he could. He jumped. And so did the hens and so did the cockerel.

⤙ 19 ⤚

Mum caught up with Betsy and Floss. She found Betsy dawdling, astonished by the beauty of everything she saw.

'Come on and stay close to me. You too, Floss. Someone's switched the sea dragon's egg for a hen's egg and it's hatched into a chick. Whoever stole the egg may be out here somewhere.'

In spite of this shocking news, Betsy was still enjoying the novelty

of being able to breathe underwater,
see underwater, and hear underwater.
Mum and Floss knew there was no
point in trying to hurry her.

They passed the jagged rocks
where the crabs and shrimps lived.
Above them, the sun glittered, making
diamonds on the water and that was
when they saw the barnacled hull of
a ship, anchored in the cove.

'That's a ship that shouldn't be
here,' said Mum.

Floss wanted to go closer to have
a better look. But Mum held him
back. On the seabed she had seen the
shadow of a wobbly figure standing
above them on a plank. Mum called
to Floss and Betsy to get
out of the way just as the
figure fell, like a stone,

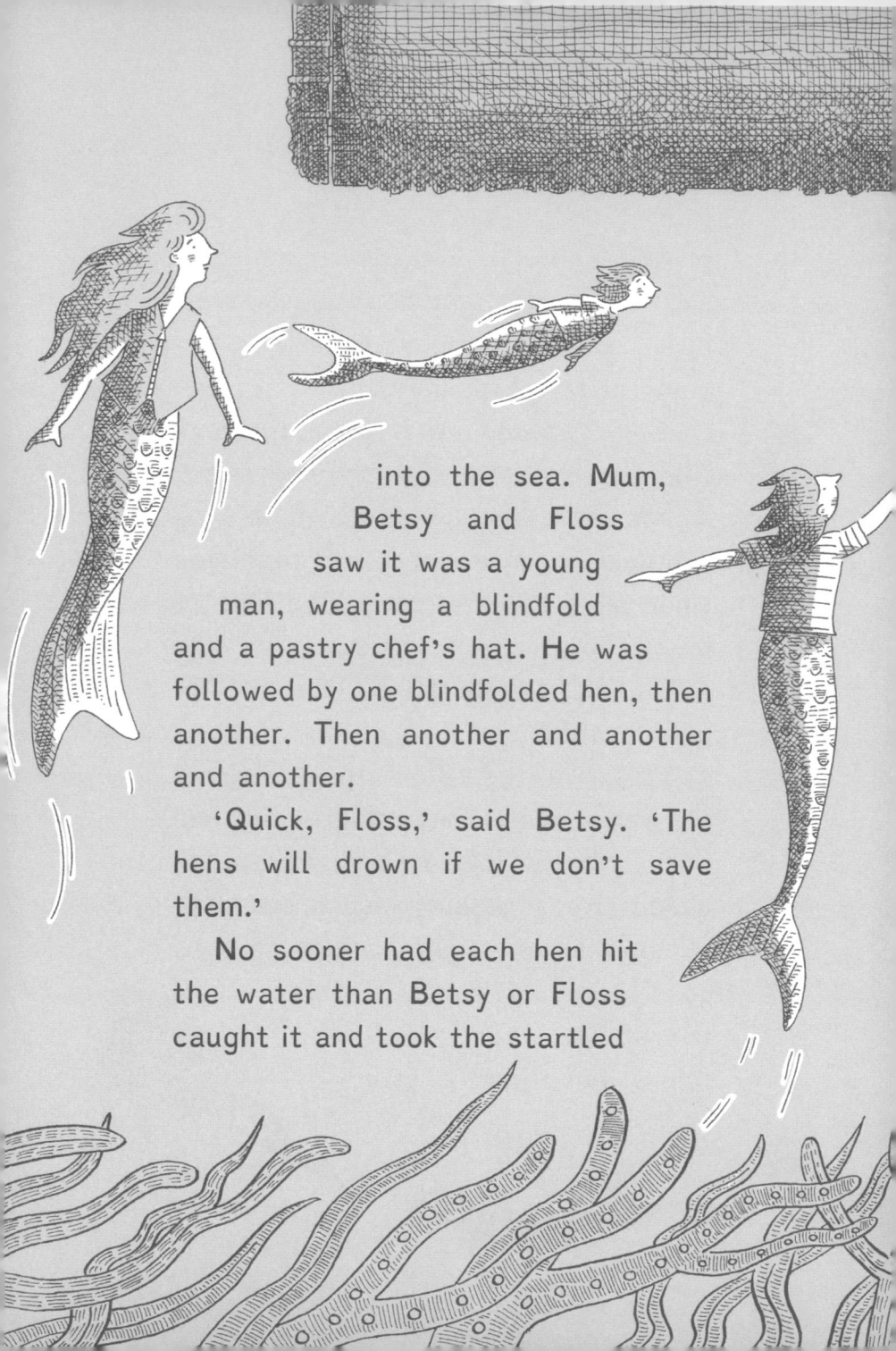

into the sea. Mum,
Betsy and Floss
saw it was a young
man, wearing a blindfold
and a pastry chef's hat. He was
followed by one blindfolded hen, then
another. Then another and another
and another.

'Quick, Floss,' said Betsy. 'The
hens will drown if we don't save
them.'

No sooner had each hen hit
the water than Betsy or Floss
caught it and took the startled

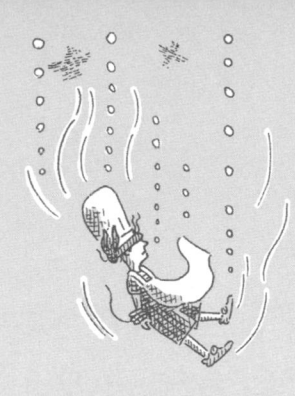

bird to shore. Luckily for Septimus, his being rather small was a great help as Mum was able to rescue him and pull him into the shallows. She untied the rope that bound his hands and from there he crawled, spluttering, on to the beach, clutching his hat to his head with one hand.

If Myrtle had been alone she would have asked him why he had been made to walk the plank. It was clear to her that it was a pirate ship he'd jumped from as it was flying a skull-and-crossbones.

The Jolly Roger, thought Mum, is

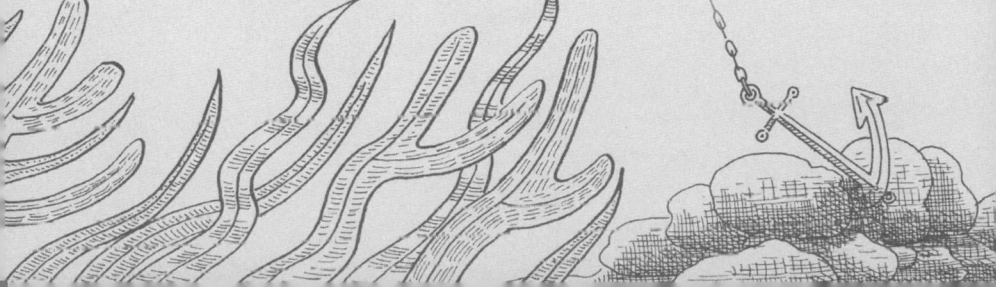

anything but jolly. And Betsy could easily be captured — she hadn't yet won her water wings.

'Come along, both of you,' said Mum, as they started to swim back to the harbour. Betsy was beginning to tire. 'Jump on, Betsy,' she said, and gave her a piggy-back all the way home.

It was only when they reached the harbour that Mum and Betsy realised Floss Grimm was nowhere to be seen.

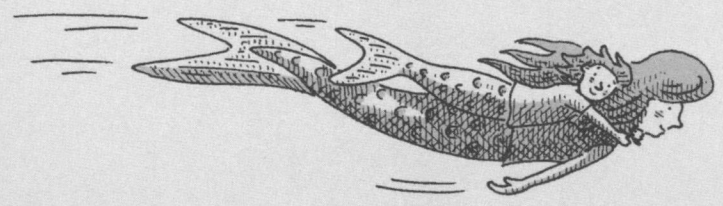

·← 20 →·

Septimus had pulled off the blindfold and wondered if he was dreaming. Had he been saved by a mermaid? He'd sat on the beach, dazed, and watched as two mer-children, one with purple hair, the other with blue hair, had rescued all his hens.

The mermaid, who also had purple hair, had called to him.

'The tide is coming in. There are steps in the third cave on the right.

They will take you to the top of the cliff.'

And with a flick of her tail she'd gone.

Septimus Plank counted his blessings and his hens. The baby sea dragon crawled out from under his hat and licked his face. Septimus decided that apart from being soaked, the baby sea dragon and the hens had suffered no ill effects. He set off up the shingle beach towards the cave that the mermaid had pointed out. The baby sea dragon sat on his shoulder and Septimus noticed that it had doubled in size since it had hatched. The hens and the cockerel followed, clucking quietly.

The cave was dark. Sticky-toffee dark. But the baby sea dragon's eyes lit up like lamps and Septimus was able to see the steps. On and on and on they went, twisting and turning in the rock. It was a slow old journey. Septimus had to keep stopping to wait for the hens, as some of them were not as sprightly as they might have been. Finally, they were rewarded with sunshine.

Septimus recognised the lane he found himself on. It was the same lane that he and Captain Calico Kettle had taken to the town hall the night they'd stolen the sea dragon's egg. He stopped by a tree, put the little sea dragon back under his pastry chef's hat and did his best to make himself look presentable. It was then he noticed, coming towards him, the same lovely lady he'd seen standing on the deck of the yacht. She was riding a small white pony and she looked as pretty as a picture, and as delicate as china cups. Septimus Plank was dumbstruck.

Princess Albee was surprised to find a handsome young man, only a little taller than she, walking down the lane surrounded by hens.

'What are you doing, walking down the lane surrounded by hens?' asked Princess Albee. 'Why are your clothes wet?'

Septimus Plank knew he should remove his hat when addressing a lady.

He whipped off his pastry chef's hat, but before he could find his voice, the lovely lady said, 'And why is there a baby sea dragon on your head?'

·← 21 →·

M r Tiger's hot–air balloon, crewed by the Gongalong acrobats, sailed into the blue sky. Dad looked down on his café by the harbour. It seemed no bigger than a doll's house.

A seagull flew past with a puzzled look on its face. Mr Tiger let out a growl and the startled seagull flew away, squawking.

'I could get used to this,' said Dad, loosening his grip on the edge of the basket. 'Oh, I can see the mayor on his balcony — still in his pyjamas. And look, there are Myrtle and Betsy in the water,' said Dad. 'But where's Floss Grimm?'

Mr Tiger took out his pocket-watch and studied it.

'There is, I fear, some worrying news concerning Floss Grimm,' he said.

'Oh, no,' said Dad. 'Not more worrying news.'

'Remember, Alfonso — brave hearts,' said Mr Tiger. 'That is what is needed. Floss Grimm has been kidnapped by pirates.'

'How do you know?' said Dad.

'Tigers have their secrets and their whiskers, their tales and their tails.'

'Oh dear,' said Dad. 'First the sea

dragon's egg is swapped for a hen's egg, and now a merboy has been captured by pirates. This is very bad indeed.'

'Onwards and upwards,' said Mr Tiger and the Gongalongs filled the balloon with another burst of hot air. This time the hot-air balloon went further out to sea but still they could not see a pirate ship anywhere. Mr Tiger studied his pocket-watch again. 'Fly us over the shoreline by the caves, if you please,' he called to the Gongalongs.

As the balloon rounded the cliffs at Pendragon Cove they spied the Kettle Black.

'We're too high up,' said Dad. 'I can't see Floss anywhere.'

'Take us down, my gutsy, gusty friends,' said Mr Tiger to the Gongalongs.

The balloon went lower until Dad could make out the pirates standing on deck, pointing up at them.

'Can you see Floss Grimm now?' asked Mr Tiger.

'No — go lower,' said Dad.

Lower still they went, and now they were close enough to see the pirate captain's wooden hand and his blue beard. He appeared to be giving orders as the pirates dashed below deck and returned with blunderbusses.

'There,' said Dad. 'In that barrel, tied to the main mast — look, it's Floss Grimm and he's waving at us.'

Mr Tiger produced a megaphone and shouted to Floss.

'Young hearts are the bravest hearts of all! Stay strong — it won't be long until we save you. Courage! Take courage, my dear young friend.'

At that moment there was a
barrage of explosions and lead shot
flew into the air, narrowly missing
the balloon.

The Gongalongs gave the balloon
several blasts of hot air and it rose

rapidly into the sky as more lead shot
came hurtling their way. It was clear
to both Mr Tiger and Dad that there
was no way they could rescue Floss
by balloon, and that another plan of
action was needed if he was going to
be saved from such savage pirates.

⊶ 22 ⊷

Betsy wriggled out of her mermaid suit on the harbour steps and left Mum in the sea while she rushed back to the café. Up the stairs of the tall, windy house she went two, three steps at a time, and into her bedroom where she quickly hung up her mermaid suit. From under her bed she grabbed the shell that she used to call Mum home, and slid down the banister all the way to the bottom.

'That must be a record,' said Mum, when Betsy returned to the harbour steps and handed her the shell. 'Tell Dad not to worry. I need to make an urgent long-distance call. I might be gone some time.'

As Mum swam away, the hot-air balloon landed by the bandstand. Betsy ran to tell Dad and Mr Tiger what had happened.

When she reached the part about the long-distance call, Mr Tiger said, 'We must tell Myrtle

where Floss Grimm
is, before she makes
that call.'

He took his megaphone from the
basket of the balloon and shouted
out to sea. His voice seemed to echo
and bounce across the water.

'MYRTLE – MYRTLE – MYRTLE
– MYRTLE.'

Mum surfaced, turned and waved
at them.

'MYRTLE, VERY IMPORTANT!

FLOSS GRIMM IS BEING HELD
CAPTIVE ON THE PIRATE SHIP IN
PENDRAGON COVE. WAVE TWICE
IF YOU READ ME.'

Mum waved twice and dived.

'Oh dear,' said Dad.

Just then a very flustered mayor
came plodding towards them trailing
bunting and carrying an official-
looking red-and-gold book.

He pointed to the sea and said,
'It's the sign. Tell me, Mr Tiger —
what do we do?'

'Brave hearts, Mr Mayor,' said
Mr Tiger firmly. 'Brave hearts. What
sign?'

Out at sea, a spout of water
exploded into the sky.

'According to the records,' said
the mayor, opening the red-and-gold

book, 'the Pap-a-naggy lets everyone know by this sign that the sea apples in the sea orchard have turned solid gold and that he is coming back to the island. This starts the second part of the Festival of the Sea Dragon.'

They all looked at the picture in the book. It showed a spout of water on the horizon.

'So tomorrow the festival will continue and the Pap-a-naggy will return for his baby,' said Mr Tiger.

'Yes,' said the mayor. 'But we don't have the baby sea dragon — we have a fluffy chick. What do we do, Mr Tiger?'

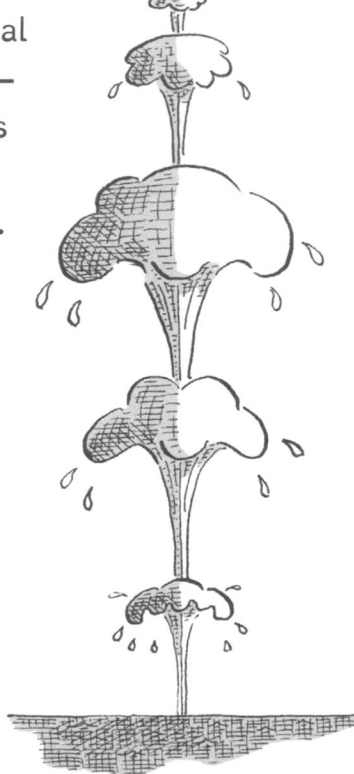

·← 23 →·

From the barrel, Floss Grimm could overhear Captain Calico Kettle and the bosun talking.

'When we get back to the map of the world,' said the captain, 'I'm going to sell that merboy for a lot of money.'

'Who will buy him?' asked the bosun.

'A zoo. Or anything that has water rides.'

'I like the way you think, Cap'n,'

said the bosun. He sighed. 'Shame the pastry chef stole the sea dragon's egg and cheated us out of them golden apples.'

The bosun and the captain had seen that Septimus Plank had somehow made it to the shore, but by the time the rowing boat had been launched to go after him, he'd vanished. That was when they'd grabbed the merboy.

Three-Legged Bill was about to go below when he spotted something on the horizon. 'Look, Cap'n — what's that out there?'

'Where?' said the captain, taking out his spyglass.

'There,' said the bosun, pointing.

'It's a water spout,' said the captain. 'Bright green and rising high into the sky.'

Floss was — in some ways — a very wise merboy and he had said nothing at all since being captured. As far as the captain knew, he couldn't speak.

'Fish can't,' he'd told Three-Legged Bill. 'And I suppose a merboy is more fish than boy.'

Floss suddenly had an idea. He knew pirates liked treasure and secrets.

He spoke slowly. 'I read in the mermaid book of old sea tales that the water spout means that tomorrow the Festival of the Sea Dragon will continue on the island.'

The captain and the bosun were awestruck.

'He speaks,' said Captain Calico Kettle. 'Speak again, merboy.'

And Floss told them that by now the sea dragon's egg would have hatched and the sea dragon would return to the island to collect his baby sea dragon and bring a golden apple.

'Just the one golden apple?' said the captain. 'Are you sure?'

The next things Floss told the captain, he made up on the spot.

'Sometimes he brings more,' said Floss.

'Does he sometimes bring crates of golden apples?' asked the captain. 'Say, three?'

'Oh, yes, sometimes,' said Floss Grimm, his fingers crossed inside the

barrel. 'Quite often, in fact. And the islanders wear fancy dress and go to the festival dressed either as an egg or a sea dragon.'

Captain Calico Kettle paced back and forth, pondering.

Finally, he summoned the crew.

'Listen up, me hearties,' he said. 'Tomorrow is our one and only chance to capture the baby sea dragon and take home three crates of golden apples — as well as a valuable merboy.'

A cheer went up from the crew.

'How are we going to do that, Captain?' asked the powder monkey.

'We are going to have to start snipping, sewing and sticking. Don't just stand there, you sissy bunch of swabs, get cracking on the eggs.'

Floss had an excellent view of the pirates as they tried to make eggs and dragons from sailcloth, ropes, nets and anything else that was lying about. At the end of the day when the pirates tried on their costumes,

he struggled to keep a straight face. Never had he seen a sillier sight. The only trouble, thought Floss, would be when Captain Calico Kettle realised that no one else on the island was in fancy dress, he'd know that Floss had lied and led him a merry dance. And things might not end well. Floss began to wonder what it would be like in a zoo.

'This is Septimus Plank,' said Princess Albee to Dad, Mr Tiger and Betsy as she sat down at the table with them in the café that afternoon. She was accompanied by a perfect, pint-sized pirate wearing a pastry chef's hat.

'Hello,' said Betsy.

She recognised him immediately as the pirate her mum had saved from drowning and she wondered if the hens were safe. She glanced under the table but she couldn't see them.

A puzzled look came over Septimus's face. He was certain that this was one of the mer-children who had rescued his hens. He too glanced under the table and saw that the little girl didn't have a mermaid's tail. But her purple hair was unmistakable.

'I think,' he said, 'I have you and your friend to thank for rescuing my hens.'

'Where are they?' asked Betsy.

'On my yacht,' said Princess Albee. 'In the stable.'

Betsy was not sure if Septimus
Plank was a good pirate or a bad
pirate but she didn't say so as she
noticed that Princess Albee had a
twinkle in her eye.

'Septimus has been incredibly
brave,' Princess Albee continued.
'Indeed, quite a hero, and he has a
story to tell.'

'A story?' Mr Tiger flashed his
white pointed teeth. 'He has a lot
of explaining to do. Who exactly is

Septimus Plank and how did he come to be a pirate? And what is a pirate doing here on an island that has been left off the map of the world?'

Septimus looked properly at Mr Tiger for the first time and nearly fell off his chair.

'W-well...' he said.

'I presume,' said Mr Tiger, 'that it has something to do with the red rogue wind?'

'Yes,' said Septimus. 'How do you know?'

'A very good question, but not one I intend to answer,' replied Mr Tiger, flexing his sharp claws and looking Septimus in the eye.

'This is most discombobulating,' said Septimus in a shaky voice.

He was trying to get his head round meeting a tiger. Meeting a tiger who could speak and was dressed in a coat and top hat.

'Discombobulating, Dad?' asked Betsy.

'It means all at odds, unsettled, a funny feeling in the tummy,' said Dad.

'Your discombobulation tells me that you are very much from the map of the world,' said Mr Tiger. 'If you weren't, you would know that I am the ringmaster of a most extraordinary circus that is named after me.'

Septimus was lost for words. He was used to a world of left and right, of A to Z, of weeks that started with Monday and years that ended on 31st December. Where a tiger was a tiger, not the ringmaster of a circus.

No wonder Septimus felt discombobulated. So very discombobulated that he had forgotten about the baby sea dragon under his hat.

'Everything here is upside down and higgledy-piggledy,' he said.

'What we all need is some refreshing ice cream,' said Dad, 'and while you're eating it, Septimus, you can tell us how you came to be a pirate.'

Dad came back with a tray of tall glasses full of his Raspberry Shiver Sparkler Delight ice cream.

'I was never a pirate,' said Septimus. 'I'm a pastry chef who got kidnapped from a cruise liner and...' He took a mouthful of ice cream, then another and another. 'Wow, this is absolutely delicious – good-beginnings and happy-ever-afters wrapped in one. It is a dream of mine to create an ice cream cake. And with this ice cream, what a cake I could create.'

'It has always been my dream to taste an ice cream cake,' said Princess Albee.

Betsy noticed that the princess blushed and she hugged the secret to herself.

At this moment Septimus's pastry chef's hat rose on his head and from under it emerged the small sea dragon. The little creature climbed

on to Septimus's shoulder, then slid
down his arm on to the table, where
it stood on its hind legs and licked
what was left of the ice cream in
Septimus's glass.

'That,' said Mr Tiger, 'is one
handsome Nog-a-naggy. And a very
healthy baby in every way. I must
congratulate you.'

Dad got some of the ice cream

he had specially made for the Pap-
a-naggy and put it on a saucer in
front of the little sea dragon. As the
sea dragon licked it all up, Septimus
finished telling his story — including
his own part in switching the eggs.

'And I stole the egg-timer,' he
added. 'Here it is.'

He took it out of his pocket and
put it on the table.

Mr Tiger growled at this, but
then put his orange-and-brown
striped paw on the young man's
shoulder and said, 'Despite your
piratical behaviour, we have much to
thank you for. If you hadn't saved
this little fellow we would have egg
on our faces. His father, the Pap-
a-naggy, will be here tomorrow to
take him back to his mother, the

Mam-a-naggy, in the sea orchard seventy leagues below the waves.'

A look of sadness passed over Septimus's face. He stroked the top of the sea dragon's head and the little creature rolled over for Septimus to rub his tummy. The sea dragon gurgled with delight.

'I will be sorry to see him go,' said Septimus. 'I have grown fond of him.'

'By the look of it,' said Dad, 'the Nog-a-naggy will miss you too.'

'Now, Septimus,' said Mr Tiger, 'it would be useful if you would tell us everything you can about the Kettle Black. Captain Calico Kettle has captured a merboy, who is Alfonso's

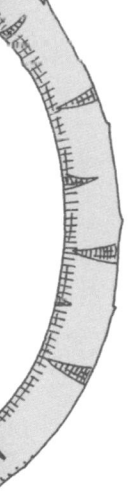

nephew, and we must hatch a plan to rescue him.'

Septimus told them all he knew and finished just as the sun threw its bathwater out into the sky before settling down to sleep.

·← 25 →·

Now, we, the letters of the alphabet are in a complete muddle as to how best to tell this part of the story because so many people weren't together who should have been.

Myrtle was somewhere in the ocean, sending a long-distance message to her sister Coral and the Siren Singers.

The pirates, dressed as eggs

and dragons and armed to the teeth,
were getting ready to raid the
island left off the map of
the world.

Floss Grimm was still in
a barrel tied to the mast
of the Kettle Black.

Princess Albee was
on her yacht, trying on her
crowns and tiaras to see
which suited her best.

Septimus Plank
was in the kitchen at
Alfonso Glory's café,
trying out ideas for an
ice cream cake that might
appeal to Princess Albee.

Mr Tiger was also at the
café, thinking over his plan.

As for Betsy, she had just climbed out of bed.

So you see, it takes a rather large piece of paper and a rather small piece of chalk and still we can't work it out. We decided our butterfly words should flutter free in the hope of giving you a glimpse of what is going on until it all comes together.

And if it doesn't come together, we will be in a real pickle. Anyway, on with the story.

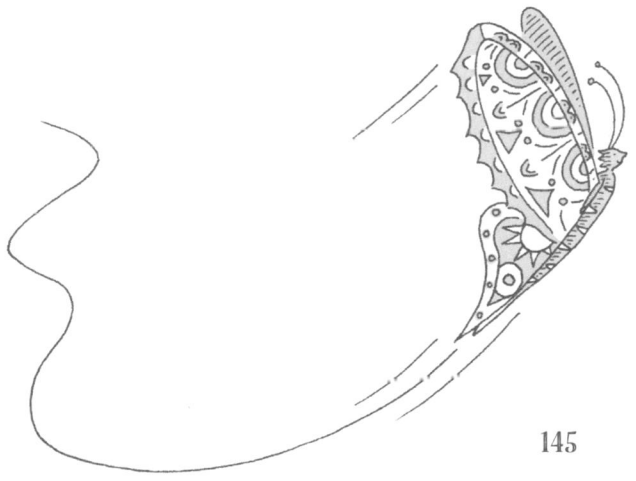

·← 26 →·

That morning, the morning of the second part of the Festival of the Sea Dragon, Mr Tiger stood at the window of the café. Septimus had asked him to keep an eye on the baby sea dragon and Mr Tiger had noted that the creature had grown considerably in the night. He was now the size of a small rabbit. Or, perhaps, a large rabbit.

Tigers often ponder and Mr Tiger was pondering how to save Floss

Grimm. He took out his pocket-watch and gazed at the pictures there. On the face appeared a picture of an egg with legs and two hands sticking out of the sides. On top of the egg sat a pirate's hat.

Grrr, thought Mr Tiger. How grrr-interesting.

He heard a thud which could only mean one thing: Betsy had landed in a heap at the foot of the stairs.

'Good morning, my sprightly one,' said Mr Tiger.

'Crumble cakes,' said Betsy, seeing the sea dragon. 'He's grown.'

'That's what sea dragons do,' said Mr Tiger, gently scratching the little sea dragon's head with his claw. He looked again at his pocket-watch. Now it showed what appeared to be

half a dozen eggs sitting in an egg box. And then he realised it was a rowing boat and that was followed by another rowing boat, this one carrying half a dozen sea dragons.

'Betsy, would you be so kind as to bring the mayor to me, he's at the harbour-master's house, advising on the bunting.'

Betsy was happy to do as he asked.

The mayor was wearing a heavy chain of office round his neck and shoes that were far too small for his feet. They were the only shiny shoes he possessed but he had read that the mayor should always wear shiny shoes for the second part of the Festival of the Sea Dragon. Even if the shiny shoes happen to be too small.

He entered the café with pinched toes, a pinched look on his face and Princess Albee on his arm. She was wearing a crown that suited her just as a crown should.

'Grand,' said Mr Tiger. 'Now, Mr Mayor,' he said. 'I believe there is to be a surprise carnival today.'

'Yes,' said the mayor. 'Some of the children have made sea dragon costumes.'

'Are there any sea dragon's eggs among them?' asked Mr Tiger.

'Yes, indeed. It's a surprise for the Pap-a-naggy. Such a relief that the Nog-a-naggy has turned up — and the egg-timer. Now I won't have to resign.'

The mayor was about to take the weight off his feet when Mr Tiger said, 'I would like you to gather the islanders by the bandstand.'

'Now?'

'Yes, now. If you please.'

The mayor hobbled away.

Mr Tiger invited the Gongalong acrobats to join him in the café. They took off their pointy hats and huddled round so they wouldn't miss a word he had to say. When the ringmaster had finished, the acrobats went away and shortly returned with ladders, a large fisherman's net, a ball of string and a lot of bunting.

'You have a plan, Mr Tiger,' said Betsy and Princess Albee together. 'We knew you would have a plan.'

+ 27 +

C aptain Calico Kettle was dressed
as an egg. He was finding it quite
hard to see out of the egg. He
was in the same awkward situation
that horses are in when blinkered. The
same went for Three-Legged Bill, the
bosun, who was also dressed as an
egg. The powder monkey was wearing
a sea dragon suit and it wasn't any
easier to see out of that. The captain
ordered all the eggs into one rowing
boat and all the sea dragons into

another and left a skeleton crew on the Kettle Black to make sure no one tried to come aboard and rescue the merboy.

It had been tricky to row a boat dressed as an egg or, for that matter, dressed as a sea dragon. The boats had gone round in several circles before the pirates were finally able to wade ashore without getting their costumes wet. Their troubles weren't over. Of course, they didn't know about the secret steps in the cave, so with great difficulty they climbed the cliff and then there was quite a way to go before they reached the town. The Gongalong acrobats were on the look-out and sprinted to Mr Glory's café to report what they had seen.

They found Mr Tiger on the
bandstand, about to make one of
his more memorable speeches. The
Gongalongs whispered the news to
him.

'Citizens of the island that has
been left off the map of the world,'
said Mr Tiger. 'I did not wish to alarm
you before, but now I need your help.
You must be brave, as I know you will
be. There is a pirate ship, the Kettle
Black, anchored in Pendragon Cove.'

'Oh, no,' cried the crowd. 'This
cannot be.'

Mr Tiger raised a paw for silence.

'Courage, my dear people, courage
is what is needed. The pirates are

coming here today dressed as eggs
and sea dragons. It is my belief that
they are on a mission to capture the
Nog-a-naggy and steal the golden
sea apple that the Pap-a-naggy will
bring you as a gift of thanks. When
they arrive in the town I want you to
act as if nothing strange is happening.
It is most important that they don't
suspect that we think them to be
anything other than islanders taking
part in the festival.'

Mrs Rose from the flower shop
raised her hand. 'How will we be able
to tell them apart from the children
appearing in the carnival?' she asked.

'The pirates are bigger, Mrs Rose,'

said Mr Tiger patiently. 'And their costumes will stand out. For example, the pirate captain's legs will be clothed in stripy breeches and there will be buckles on his shoes. He will wear a pirate's hat on the top of his egg costume. In other words, they will not be hard to spot. We must guide them all into Mr Glory's café and once they are there, the Gongalongs and I will know what to do. Brave hearts, my friends, are what I want from you today if we are to save this island from these greedy pirates.'

'Here they come,' called the Gongalong acrobats.

'Remember — brave hearts! And act as if nothing is wrong,' said Mr Tiger.

·✦ 28 ·✦

Myrtle had made contact with her sister Coral, and Coral and the Siren Singers had swum swiftly to the island left off the map of the world. Myrtle met them on the seabed in Pendragon Cove, below the hull of the Kettle Black.

'No matter what we sing,' said Coral, 'we can't reach Floss without someone who has legs.'

'Yes,' said Myrtle. 'I've thought of

that. Stay here and I will be back in a jiffy.'

With a flick of her tail, she turned and swam to the harbour as fast as she could. She arrived as Mr Tiger finished his speech and was returning to the café. Dad was so relieved to see her.

'I'm not stopping, Alfonso,' said Mum. 'Call Betsy and tell her to bring her mermaid suit. She's coming with me to help rescue Floss Grimm.'

'Is that a good idea?' said Dad.

'It's the only idea I have.'

Dad looked round to see several wobbly eggs on legs and wonky sea dragons arriving in town. They looked anything but friendly.

Dad walked calmly into the café.

'Betsy, the pirates are here,' he said. 'And Mum is waiting for you at the harbour steps. She wants you to help save Floss. Quickly, get your mermaid suit.'

'Crumble cakes — an adventure!' said Betsy and rushed upstairs, grabbed her mermaid suit and slid down the banister without landing in a heap, for a change. She stopped and realised that, for the first time, she felt scared. Mr Tiger, who had just arrived at the café, asked what the matter was.

'We have always been on adventures together,' said Betsy. 'Couldn't you come with me? My tummy feels full of little fearful fishes.'

Mr Tiger kneeled down, which
he had never done before, until his
magnificent head was at the same
height as Betsy's. His golden eyes
looked straight into hers. Betsy felt
sure he could even see the little
fearful fishes in her tummy.

'Tigers,' he said, 'can swim, but

they can't breathe underwater. Betsy K Glory, you are the bravest girl I have ever known. You can do this.' Then he lifted her up and gave her a hug.

The smell of his fur, Betsy decided, was the most comforting smell she knew. It was enough to make her feel brave. She would not let Mr Tiger or Mum down.

Betsy was about to run out of the café when the door was flung open and a wobbly egg wearing a pirate's hat came in.

'Are you part of the festivities?' said the egg to Mr Tiger.

'Indubitably,' said Mr Tiger.

'What language is that, then?' said Captain Calico Kettle, whose voice was somewhat scrambled by the egg costume.

'English,' said Mr Tiger. 'It means without a doubt.'

'Shiver me rotting timbers. Why didn't you say so? Now, is this the café that sells ice cream?'

'Yes, it is,' said Dad.

'And today the ice cream is free for anyone dressed as a sea dragon or an egg,' added Mr Tiger.

'Give me a taste,' said Captain Calico Kettle. 'I can't trust someone in fancy dress, who uses fancy words like "indubitably".'

'What flavour would you like?' asked Dad.

'You mean — you have more flavours than just vanilla?'

'Indubitably,' said Dad. 'We have Raspberry Ribble Wonder, Chocolate Toffee Delight, Lemon Sugar Shocker, Strawberry Sparklers, Popping Peanut Plenties, Myrtle's Minty Mumbo Marvel, Chocolate Cherry Delight and Knickerbocker...'

And while Dad was reciting the menu, Betsy and Mr Tiger slipped out.

The tide was with them and Betsy and Mum reached the seabed under the Kettle Black in double-quick time. Betsy was surprised to see so many mermaids gathered there.

'Hello, Betsy — my, oh, my, what a suit,' said Aunty Coral, whose hair was lime yellow. 'Why, sis, I didn't think you had it in you to knit such a piece of sea magic. I'm glad you haven't forgotten the ways of the Shell.'

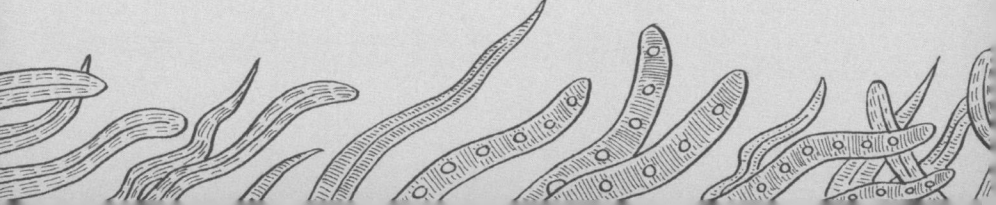

'The Shell is mermaid-speak for home,' murmured Mum.

'Oh,' said Betsy, a little nervously.

She hadn't imagined Aunty Coral being so sharp.

'I speak with shark's teeth,' said Aunty Coral. 'But my heart is as soft as a jellyfish. Welcome, Betsy. Now, we don't know how many pirates are on board and whether they will all fall asleep so we sent the turtles to call for back-up. Sisters,' she said, turning to the other mermaids, 'if we are ready, then let us begin.'

And they started to sing.

·← 30 →·

On the deck of the Kettle Black, the pirates who had been left behind had helped themselves to a tot of rum and were playing cards. They were in a merry mood — the kind of mood you're in when you know the boss is away and you won't get told off for being naughty.

They were thinking about going down to the galley for a snack when they heard singing. It was such beautiful song — high in pitch, and tinkling as wind chimes do. The voices sang of a longing for home and bed. The pirates listened and thought of their mums, they thought of their families and the days before they became rascally seadogs. As they listened, they began to feel rather sleepy, until they could hardly keep their eyes open. And soon they were all curled up, dreaming of being small and safe.

Mum helped Betsy take off her mermaid costume so she could climb the rope ladder up on to the deck.

Once on deck, Betsy felt brave. There was not one little fearful fish in her tummy. She imagined that Mr Tiger was with her as she tiptoed past the sleeping pirates and was very glad to see Floss Grimm safe and sound. Floss Grimm was very glad to see Betsy as he was fed up with being in a barrel. He was rather less glad when Betsy told him his mum was below waiting for him.

Betsy was wondering how to help Floss out of the barrel and into the sea when something happened. Something so unexpected that she couldn't make head nor tail of it. The

Kettle Black tilted at such a steep angle that Betsy was only saved from sliding all the way down to the stern by clinging to the mast.

'Oh, crumble cakes,' she said. 'This doesn't feel good.'

Floss held tight to the edge of the barrel as water poured out of it. Then the Kettle Black straightened itself and rose so high out of the sea that it was sailing on the clouds. The pirates stayed sound asleep.

Cautiously, Betsy looked over the side.

'The ship is being held out of the water by a huge sea dragon,' she said. 'I don't remember the Pap-a-naggy being so ginormous when I last saw him. Do you think he's grown?'

'Or maybe,' said Floss, 'it's the Mam-a-naggy. She's supposed to be really huge.'

'But she never leaves the sea apple orchard.'

'I suppose there's a first time for everything.'

'Oh, double crumble cakes,' said Betsy. 'Do you speak Tangerine?'

'A bit,' said Floss. 'Mum isn't keen on it.'

'I don't think that matters at this moment. The Mam-a-naggy must be the back-up that your mum told the turtles to fetch. Tell her we are here.'

'!•?#¢!' said Floss in Tangerine.

No reply.

'Hallo, Mam-a-naggy — we're up here, you blithering two-eyed monster from the deep. We are not, repeat not, pirates.'

'Tell her that her egg hatched and her baby is safe,' said Betsy.

'Your egg hatched,' said Floss as best he could in Tangerine. 'You have a bonny, bouncing baby sea dragon.'

Suddenly, a huge eye was peering at them. The eye came closer, followed by a head and a talon, and then the Mam-a-naggy scooped up a sleeping pirate, dangled him before her and swallowed him whole. A thoughtful look came over her features and she let out a loud belch. The pirate, covered in slime and still sleeping, landed back on deck.

'Rotten is it he tastes,' said the Mam-a-naggy.

'Pirates are not for eating,' said Floss.

'Ask her if she would kindly take us back to the harbour,' said Betsy.

'Tangerine is a pithy language,' said Floss. 'It's meant to be spoken rudely.'

'Try "please", just for a change,' said Betsy.

'Take us back to the harbour, you great burping ball of blubber,' said Floss. 'Please.'

Mr Tiger had returned to the café after seeing Betsy off. His plan was simple: to tempt the pirates into a trap with free ice cream. And it wasn't long before all the pirate eggs and pirate sea dragons were jostling to get into the café. Alfonso was busy serving them.

Captain Calico Kettle took off his hat and sat down. Never had he tasted anything as delicious as Alfonso's ice cream. He and the

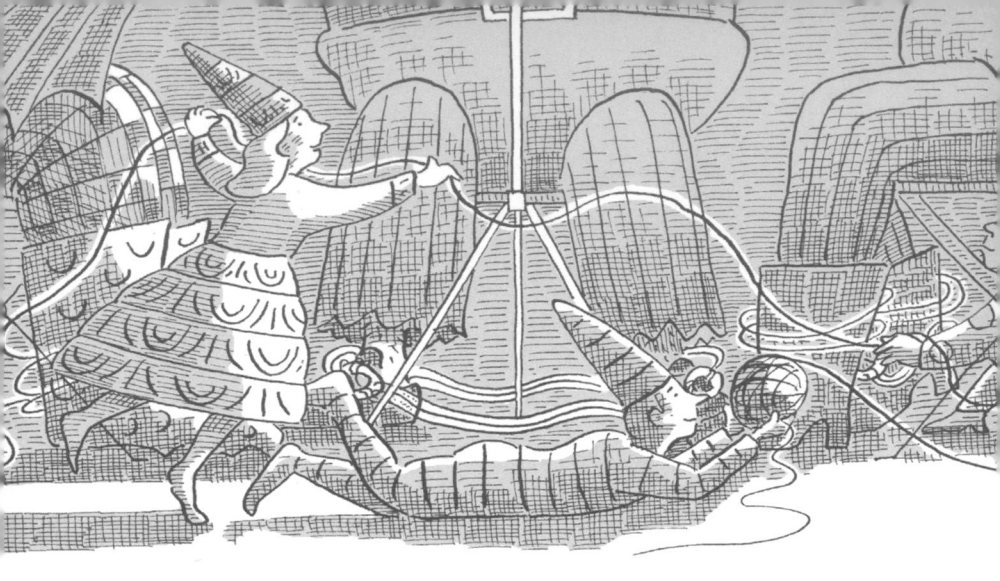

other pirates wanted to sample every flavour. By the time they had licked their spoons clean, the Gongalongs had unrolled the ball of string and quietly tied the pirates together by their boot buckles and wooden legs.

Meanwhile, other Gongalongs slid in unseen and waited for Mr Tiger to give them the sign.

It was only when Captain Calico Kettle had finished his sixth flavour — Myrtle's Minty Mumbo Marvel

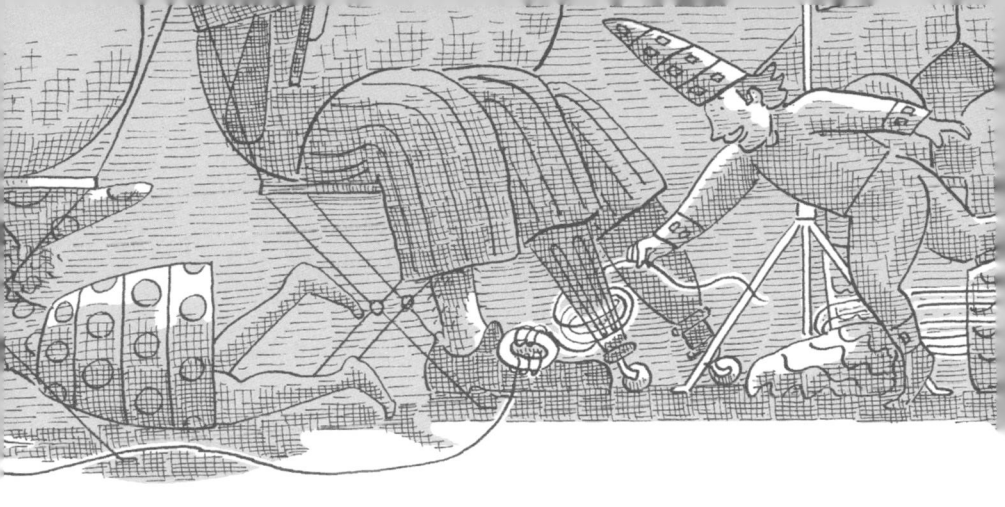

— that he found he couldn't move. For a moment he thought it might be something to do with eating so much ice cream. But then he realised that he and his crew were spliced to one another. With difficulty, he took out his pistol from under his egg costume and pointed it at Mr Tiger.

'Untie our boots,' he bellowed, 'or you'll end up as a rug on my cabin floor.'

Dad ducked behind the counter

and Mr Tiger let
out a terrifying roar.

Just then the mayor burst into the
café in his socks, whirling his chain
of office. He brought it down hard
on Captain Calico Kettle's egg-head.
The egg cracked and the captain
wobbled to and fro, before crashing
to the floor.

Mr Tiger raised his paw, the
Gongalongs released the fisherman's

net and bunting from the ceiling and down they fell, completely covering the pirates. Alfonso, Septimus, the mayor and the Gongalongs made sure not a single pirate escaped.

But screams and shouts could be heard outside — people were running past the café crying, 'Look, look!'

Mr Tiger looked. Swimming into the mouth of the harbour was an enormous sea dragon, escorted by a flotilla of mermaids.

'It's the Mam-a-naggy,' said Mr Tiger. 'And she's carrying the Kettle Black. It seems Betsy has done a splendid job of rescuing Floss Grimm without me.'

·←· 32 ·→·

The pirates could not escape the Gongalong acrobats who guarded them. And, fortunately, as the Gongalongs didn't speak Tangerine, they had no idea how rude the pirates were being.

Princess Albee may have looked as delicate as a china cup, but she really was as strong as cement. She calmed the islanders, saying no one was to worry, they were safe and the Mam-a-naggy wouldn't come any closer.

She stepped forward to welcome the Pap-a-naggy who had squeezed into the harbour and was waiting at the quayside.

Mr Tiger joined her.

'Dear Pap-a-naggy, welcome. We are pleased to tell you that your baby sea dragon has hatched and the Nog-a-naggy is a very bonny sea dragon indeed.'

Septimus walked to the edge of the quay, cuddling the Nog-a-naggy. The Pap-a-naggy stood on his hind legs, towering over Septimus, then reached out with his front talons and carefully took the sleeping young sea dragon from him. The Pap-a-naggy began to speak in Tangerine.

Myrtle, who had just swum up to the quayside, with Coral and the Siren

Singers, translated for the islanders.

'He says,' said Myrtle, '"Oh, my beastie boy, my perfect beamish baby," — I think that's right — "what a dream-ish dragon, what a Nog-a-naggy you are."'

The people of the town cheered and cheered.

The Pap-a-naggy continued speaking.

'Me and my beastie other half thank you, all you little nuts on legs. From three rotten solid gold apples that are hardly worth twinkle, let alone a thank you, what can we do for you?'

Myrtle did her best to give the zest of his speech to the islanders. Then in reply she told the Pap-a-naggy about the pirates and how they had stolen the egg, and kidnapped her nephew, Floss Grimm, and that he and her daughter, Betsy, were on board the pirate ship that his missus was holding.

'We would be so grateful, you great scaly sea slug,' said Myrtle, 'if we could have our children back. And perhaps you and the Mam-a-naggy would remove the pirates from the island.'

'Very well said,' said Coral to her sister.

The Pap-a-naggy stared at his sleeping infant. When he looked up his eyes flashed red with anger.

'One thing is there hate I,' said the Pap-a-naggy, 'and that be salty sea dogs smelly shanty pirates.'

He shouted to the mouth of the harbour where the Mam-a-naggy was still clutching the Kettle Black in her huge talons.

'Bring out the pirates,' Myrtle said to Mr Tiger, 'so that the Pap-a-naggy can see them.'

The Gongalong acrobats, being many and strong, carried the parcel of netted pirates down to the quay.

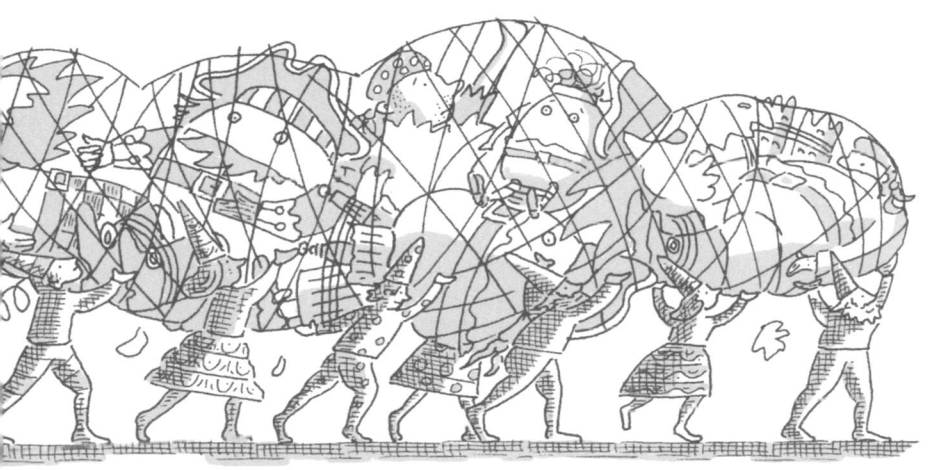

'Oh, my trembling timbers,' said Captain Calico Kettle, peering out of his cracked-egg costume at the Pap-a-naggy. 'We are properly fried, me hearties.'

The Pap-a-naggy gave the Nog-a-naggy back to Septimus to hold while he dealt with the pirates. He picked up the net and, carefully, so as not to damage any boats in the harbour, waded, then swam, out to the Mam-a-naggy, dragging the net behind him while the pirates squealed and said bad words in Tangerine. He dropped the netful of pirates on to the Kettle Black and gently picked up

first Betsy, then Floss Grimm in his talons and returned to the harbour where Myrtle and Coral were waiting for their children.

As everyone on the quayside watched, the Mam-a-naggy puffed up her cheeks and blew so hard on the sails of the Kettle Black that the ship skimmed like a pebble back to the map of the world. The cheers from the islanders woke the little Nog-a-naggy and, seeing his mother, he squeaked and wriggled free from Septimus. Flapping his wings, he took to the water — and immediately sank. His father fished him up and they both joined the Mam-a-naggy.

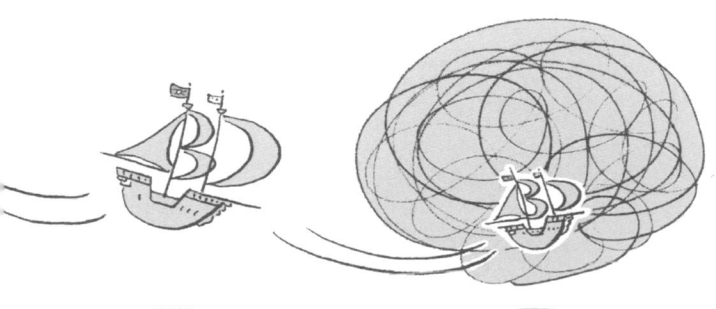

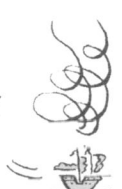

Accompanied by many shouts and much throwing of hats and choruses of, 'For he's a jolly good fellow,' the family returned to their sea apple orchard seventy leagues below the waves. It was only when they had gone that the mayor realised that three crates of golden apples had been left on the quay. One golden apple for each islander who lived off the map of the world.

⠀⠢⠀ 33 ⠀⠔⠀

We, the letters of the alphabet, noticed something and you most probably did too. And that something is Septimus Plank. He didn't leave with the pirates and any hope he might have had of being returned to the map of the world was gone. Yet we have to say, if he was upset about it, he never showed it, not one bit. He went straight back to the café and into the kitchen.

That day was unlike any other day.

It was a grand celebration kind of day, the kind that when you're feeling blue, you dream of. All its hours were brimming with entertainment. Princess Albee was rather sad that Septimus wasn't with her to enjoy it.

Mr Tiger saw she was glum and said, 'Smile, my dear princess, because tonight there will be a surprise waiting.'

You may also want to know what happened to Floss Grimm when he was reunited with his mum. Now here's a funny thing. Coral was cross with him

for being so naughty but somehow all that crossness changed to relief and relief turned into joy at having him safe. He told her that he was very, very sorry and promised he would never swim away again. Myrtle added that Floss had shown great courage in saving the hens and Betsy said he'd been helpful in teaching her how to swim underwater.

That evening there was a banquet. Oh, you should have seen it. But wait — for of course you can.

All the tables were laid out by the harbour where the Gongalongs had strung paper lanterns on wires that reached the stars. The moon peered down to see what was going on, for it was fond of a circus. Coral and the Siren Singers gave a concert, and as the stars shone, the Gongalongs performed their acrobatics before joining the islanders for the banquet.

Mum sat next to Dad with her tail in a bucket. Dad sat next to Betsy who sat next to Mr Tiger. Mr Tiger sat next to Princess Albee. Princess Albee sat next to Septimus and both looked very happy. Princess Albee wore another tiara and Betsy wore her golden seahorse, which gleamed on the chain around her neck.

At the end of the meal, Septimus

went into the café
and brought out
an ice cream
cake that he
had made
especially for
Princess Albee. Iced
on the top was a heart.

Princess Albee blushed.

'I created it for you, with all my love,' said Septimus.

Princess Albee ate a spoonful of the ice cream cake.

'It tastes of happy-ever-afters,' she said, looking at Septimus.

'Crumble cakes,' said Betsy. 'Are you two going to get married? Can I be a bridesmaid? Oh, I really like the idea of a royal wedding.'

Princess Albee smiled and took

Septimus's hand. 'So do I,' she said.

Before the princess could say another word, Mr Tiger stood up to give a speech.

'Ladies and gentlemen, brave hearts all, we can sleep easy in our beds this night knowing the island is safe.' The islanders applauded. 'Furthermore, it has been decided by the mayor and Princess Albee that something must be done to help Myrtle and Alfonso Glory have a more mer-friendly house.'

'Hear hear, and about time too,' cried the islanders.

'Tomorrow, work will begin on the house and café. Waterslides, water lifts, waterbeds and everything else the modern mermaid might need will be installed. I raise my glass to...'

'To another adventure together?' Betsy whispered.

'To another adventure together,' said Mr Tiger. He took out his pocket-watch and studied it. 'Well, frazzle my whiskers, it looks as if something exciting is coming this way.'

'Are you sure?' asked Betsy.

'Sure,' said Mr Tiger. 'A hundred Gongalongs sure.'

'How do you know?' said Betsy.

'Because, Betsy K Glory, tigers have their secrets and their whiskers, their tails and their tales.'

Out now in paperback!

MR TIGER, BETSY
and the
BLUE MOON

Read the first book in Sally Gardner's
enchanting new series, illustrated by
Nick Maland.

When Betsy K Glory, the daughter of
a mermaid and an ice cream maker,
meets the mysterious Mr Tiger they
have a giant challenge... a moon to
turn blue, berries to collect and
wishable-delicious ice cream to
create. The sort that makes
wishes come true.

Crumble cakes!

MR TIGER, BETSY
and the
GOLDEN SEAHORSE

Coming in Spring 2020

Mr Tiger and Betsy join Myrtle to listen
to tall tales from her world beneath
the waves. There may be monsters...
shipwrecks, lost treasure and secret
cities. But what happens when a tiger's
whiskers and tail are simply too long
to squeeze into forgotten dark caverns
where even the moon cannot shine, and
Betsy has to take the final steps of the
adventure on her own?

Author's Note

My great hope is that all the books in the series will be accompanied by a big brass band, and I feel confident in saying that big brass band will keep on booming. I have thoroughly loved writing this book and it is a joy to return to these characters. Once again it is being published in blue and in Dyslexie font.

I would like to thank Fiona Kennedy, Jessie Price and Clémence Jacquinet at Zephyr; my assistant, Amelia Barratt for her unbelievable patience and good humour; the effervescent Jacky Bateman; Freya Corry for her wisdom and to Nick Maland for his fabulous illustrations. This book would not be the same without his vision.

Lastly I'd like to say: Imagination is a unicorn of the mind. You need to feed it and care for it every day to make it become a thing of wonder. Imagination is the greatest gift any child is born with and I believe we need to nurture it, not crush it with examinations. The only way to make it grow is through story, through play, through believing the impossible to be real and making it so.

Sally Gardner
Sussex, May 2019

At Zephyr we are proud to publish books
you can read and re-read time and time
again because they tell a brilliant story
and because they entertain you.

Subscribe to our newsletter to hear all
the latest news about upcoming releases,
competitions and to have the chance to
win signed books. Just drop us a line at
hello@headofzeus.com

 @_ZephyrBooks

 HeadofZeus

WWW.HEADOFZEUS.COM

ZEPHYR

Tomorrow's classics today